DARICE BAILER AND

ROSEMARIE MOLSER

COMES A
LITTLE LIGHT

DREAM HOUSE BOOKS. Miami, Florida

Requests for permission to make copies of any part of the work should be mailed
to the following address: Permissions Department, DreamHouse Books, Inc., 1405
West 24th Street, Sunset Island III, Miami Beach, FL 33140

www.dreamhousebooks.com

Library of Congress Cataloging –in-Publication Data
Bailer, Darice.
Comes A Little Light/Darice Bailer
1. World War, 1939-1945-Fiction2. World War, 1939-1945-Germany-Fiction.
3. Germany-History-1933-1945-Fiction. 4. Holocaust, Jewish (1939-1945)-Fiction.
5. German American women-Fiction. 6. Young women-Fiction.
ISBN 978-1-60530-442-7

Text set in Adobe Caslon Pro
Designed by Jennifer Jackman

Printed in the United States of America

First DreamHouse Books edition 2008

To my parents, Gertrude and Julius Marienthal, who helped me become who I am. It was my mother who gave me my love for music and beautiful things, and it was my father who passed on his sense of right and wrong and showed me that it was important to find the courage to speak up when something was wrong.

To my sister Margrit, for her devotion to saving our parents and Heidi at great personal sacrifice. I miss you both.

To my daughter Kathy, my son Bruce, my grandchildren and my great grandchildren for enriching my life.

And, most of all, to my husband. You helped me grow up, and I helped you grow old.

R.M.M.

Several years ago, my mother said, "Why don't you call my friend Rosemarie? She's working on a book, and maybe you could help her."

That was the beginning of a relationship that was "beshert," a Yiddish word meaning destined to be. While interviewing Rosemarie for this book, I learned that she had recently lost her beloved daughter Kathy, that Kathy had been helping her write her Holocaust memoir, and that Kathy and I were very close in age. I picked up where Kathy left off, and the friendship grew.

Rosemarie and I talked about books and movies, politics and war. We also talked about her life, in every detail. Rosemarie not only shared her story with me, but all of her family's letters and poems. And when we finished the book, Rosemarie asked that I forward the letters on to Germany, to be stored in a museum, but I couldn't part with them. The letter writers – she and her family – meant too much to me to let them go.

This book is dedicated to Rosemarie and the Marienthal family, and is in memory of Tante Johanna and Uncle Phillip.

D.B.

Whenever you think you can't go on anymore
Comes a little light from somewhere,
And if you overcome once more
And sing of sunshine and joy
You can carry the tough load that you have to carry
And gain strength and courage and faith.

By Julius Marienthal
Translated from the German

Heidi and Rosemarie

The Golden Hour

Memories surface from the past
to hold a dialogue with us in stillness
Pleading to bring us back to the Parkstrasse.
The door opens and three flowers stand next to our bed.
Margrit, Rosemarie and Heidi recite a joyous poem in soaring trio.
The gong sounds!
Now we are cheerfully assembled
Near the lamp's white glow.
Harmony!
Oh, to hold on to the golden hour,
the house of three maidens.
Could it ever have been more beautiful?
Now it is all gone,
for we were expelled from memory's paradise.

The farewell is hard to bear.
We had to part
from the homeland and home,
from property and possession.
But to what avail are complaints and lamentations?
We should not grumble, for
from this loss greater joy may still come our way.

And so with courage and faith
we calmly tread onto the new world.
We are free from oppression, free from the persecution mania.
We will rise again,
from gloomy night to light.
Steep is the path,
but we will continue to strive,
glad to be in our home again.

By Julius Marienthal Translated from the German

CHAPTER ONE

Rosemarie (left), Heidi and Margrit

I WANTED A LETTER that day in boarding school
and I got one. Sister Katherine waved it in front of me after I
sat down to dinner in the dining hall. The note was cloaked in a
beige onion skin envelope, and Sister Katherine could not hide her
excitement as she handed out the daily mail.

"Rosemarie," Sister Katherine said in her black habit, with the
dark paneled walls of the room behind her. "There's a letter for you
today. And, it's from Africa!"

Africa? Who would write me from Africa? My classmates
looked up at me and stared in the dining hall, waiting to hear the
answer. Tree branches were bare skeletons against the setting sun
outside. Inside, the mahogany benches were still. Not a fork lifted.
Not a hand stirred.

"Here you are!" said Sister Katherine as she handed me her
mysterious present, her forehead creased with a smile. Steam rose
from the dish on my tray, and my face flushed warm and red as I felt
each pair of questioning eyes.

I examined the stamp with its picture of a carved wooden mask as a few of my friends rose and gathered around me. "Rosemarie, who is it?" "Who wrote you?" "Who's your new boy friend?" "Open it. Quick!"

There were no e-mails, text messages, or cell phones back then. In 1938, I lived for the mail, especially for a letter written by a dear familiar hand from home. My older sister Margrit wrote about Bochum and our friends in Germany, and my younger sister Heidi told me about carrying her books past the Reichstag on her way to photography class in Berlin. My friends Gert Freudenberg and Suzi Zucker wrote me, too. I never heard from my non-Jewish friends, though. They had been silent ever since I was kicked out of school back home.

I slipped my index finger into the back of the envelope and tore it open quizzically as my classmates flocked around and peered over my shoulder. The letter was typewritten on the barest, thinnest stationery. The paper was almost as sheer as tissue paper, and so delicate that the keystrokes punched holes through it. The letter was single-spaced, and there was only a sliver of a border without ink. I always double-spaced my papers for class, and had never seen so many typed words on one sheet of paper.

2 October, 1938

Dear Miss Marienthal,

Your uncle, Phillip Guttentag, gave me your name and suggested that I write you. I know it must be funny for you to receive a letter from a stranger, but let me explain. I am a new doctor here in the Belgian Congo, and I met Mr. Guttentag a while back in Berlin. He was one of my patients and has been like a fatherly friend ever since.

What am I doing in the Congo, you wonder? Well, I was kicked out of the University of Berlin in 1933 with all of my Jewish friends after completing my medical studies. The Nazis felt they had far too many Jewish doctors for their liking.

Luckily I found work as a physician in Africa, first in a gold mine and now in my own practice. It was sad to say good-bye to my friends and colleagues at the university, and it was especially hard to say good-bye to my parents whom I love dearly. I am an only child and I am all that they have. They are all that I have as well.

It is lonely here in Africa, and Mr. Guttentag gave me your name. I wonder if we might write each other now and then and get to know each other a little better. Perhaps you miss your family and friends back in Germany the way I do. Maybe we have that in common.

I am 30 and in all likelihood much older than you. In any case, Mr. Guttentag wouldn't tell me your age. He just said that you would one day catch up with me! I hope that you will write me back and that perhaps we can be pen pals. I would love to hear more about you and about your school.

All the best wishes,
Herbert Molser
Stanleyville, Belgian Congo

The letter was not from Gert. My heart always beat a little faster whenever I saw my name written in Gert's scribbly handwriting. Sometimes his words slanted straight up and sometimes they raced forward. Gert's writing looked as awkward as he did, as we both did together.

I handed the letter to Sophie, one of my classmates, and I watched Sophie's green eyes move down the page as she read. If this was one of my papers, my English teacher would have lowered my grade for not skipping lines and leaving appropriate margins.

My friend Kathe crowded next to Sophie, reading along with her, and then Sophie gasped. "It's from a 30-year-old MAN!" she said.

Precisely.

"That is so ancient!" Kathe exclaimed, after finishing the last paragraph.

Kathe was right.

"What kind of 30-year-old doctor," Sophie said, waving the letter in front of her, "tries to make friends with a 17-year-old girl?"

It was peculiar, I had to agree. "You know, we could have some fun with this," Kathe said aloud, staring at the ceiling,

"You mean answer it?" Sophie asked.

"Like together!" said Kathe.

I had to laugh. It would be something Inge would think of, one of my old friends from school. Inge would have some witty things to say to this doctor, this sophisticated man from Berlin who was nearly twice my age. I grabbed the letter out of Sophie's hand. "We could answer this old doctor's letter so that he wouldn't ever think about writing to me again!"

That is how we gathered on my bed that evening in our dormitory, my classmates and I. It was like my last school trip back home, the time we stayed over night in a youth hostel in the mountains not far from Bochum. My friends Inge, Doris, Crystal and I grabbed beds next to each other, and chatted late into the night about our teacher, Herr Wenzel, and his girl friend, our gym teacher.

There were no letters from Gert or my friends in Bochum today, but there was this letter from Africa, and everyone had a say in what we wrote that night. Each of us added a line or two, and we tried to be as outrageous and insulting as we could.

9 October 1938

Dear Dr. Molser,

I have untied my braids tonight so that I can write to you. The braces

*on my teeth came out last summer in Bochum, although the dentist didn't
do too good a job because I've still got buck teeth.*

*It's lots of fun here at Catholic school. We like to spit out our gum in
mass and stick it on the back of our hymn books so that the next person
who comes along will get sticky fingers...*

My friends dictated one mocking line after another. We teased
Dr. Molser about growing bald and gaining a middle-aged pouch. It
was amusing at first, but then my conscience stirred and clucked its
tongue, and I stopped writing and tore the letter in half.

"Hey, what are you doing?" Sophie asked, blinking her green
eyes at me. "It was just getting good!"

"Well," I said. "Even if this Dr. Molser is old, he's probably
lonely down there in Africa, and we all know how it feels to be on
our own, away from our home and families. Not to mention in a
foreign country. You were all very funny, but I don't think I could
ever send a letter like this. Even if this man is ancient, it isn't right."

"Oh Rosemarie, you are too nice," Kathe said, flopping back on
her bed. "Watch. You'll probably end up marrying the guy!"

"I don't think so," I said, as I flicked off the light and settled
under my blanket, adjusting my long flannel gown around my legs.
"You're forgetting about Gert."

I'd known Gert Freudenberg since Judische Volkschule, or the
Jewish school that I attended. In the area of Germany where I lived,
children were required to begin their education at a school affiliated
with their church or synagogue, and I began the Judischvolkschule
in first grade in a building next to our synagogue in the center of
Bochum. When I was in fifth grade, my parents enrolled me in a
private girls school where I met Inge.

I often wondered who was smarter, Gert or Inge. Gert was
brilliant, especially in math. He would help me with my math

homework at his apartment, which was up the hill and around the corner from my house. Gert and I both liked to read, and we would exchange books and talk about them together on our walks. I always hoped Gert would invite me to the movies so that we could become more than just friends.

I said good-bye to Gert when I was kicked out of school after calling the Nazis "barbarians" following another one of their restrictions against the Jews. It was the wrong thing to say to Inge, especially since her uncle was the famous Red Baron, the pilot who shot down 80 enemy planes during the war. Inge told her father, and somehow the Gestapo found out and called my father in to headquarters. "You had better teach your daughter to show more respect for the Fuhrer," the Gestapo warned.

My parents decided that it was too dangerous for me to stay in Germany, so my mother wrote to a dozen boarding schools, hoping to find one that would take me. Switzerland was the logical place for me to go, since German was the official language, and luckily Mother Superior didn't hesitate to admit me.

After all, her savior had been a Jew.

So, here I was, singing Ave Maria and dreaming about Gert. Of course I'd be polite and write back to that doctor, but I tried to remember everything about Gert before I fell asleep that night. The dark lock of hair that dipped over his eyebrow, his shy smile, and the navy blazer he always wore to school. Maybe, when I returned home, he'd finally ask me to the movies and hold my hand.

CHAPTER TWO

Rosemarie

A FEW WEEKS LATER, Sister Marlena tapped me on the shoulder. "Mother Superior would like to see you in her office," she said, and before I could question her, she was gone and I was left staring at the back of her cape.

It was October 20, 1938, and the fact that Mother Superior asked to meet me that day worried me. She hardly ever summoned anyone to her office since she could speak with us herself after chapel. Was it the B on my last Latin test, or did my mind sometimes wander in Mass? The truth was, though, I recited the Mass in Latin as well as my Christian peers now, and, I was good at memorizing the weekly Bible verse.

Trust in the Lord, and in all ways acknowledge him, and He will direct your path.

I knocked on Mother Superior's heavy paneled door, letting my higher power direct me, and in seconds I heard the grandmotherly voice I knew so well.

"Come in, Rosemarie," Mother Superior said.

"You asked to see me?" I said, hesitating at the threshold.

"Yes, Rosemarie, but my dear, I can see the look of concern on your face! Sit down! " she said, motioning me forward. "You have done nothing wrong!"

I sat down in a black leather chair in front of Mother Superior's desk and waited for her to begin. "Rosemarie, your parents have requested that you come home."

Come home? I knew that the situation for Jews was getting worse in Germany, not better. My parents couldn't write me and tell me because the Nazis would cut out those paragraphs or draw a thick blue line through the handwriting. I read everything in the Swiss newspaper, though, which wasn't filled with Nazi propaganda like the papers back home. I knew how the Nazis demanded that Jews register their homes, silver and valuables, and how the Germans had started taking over Jewish homes and auctioning them off to Gentiles.

The anti-Jewish decrees had not subsided either. In June, my uncle, a doctor, had been told he could only treat Jews, and a month later he lost his license and couldn't practice medicine at all. Then, a few months ago, my parents and sisters were ordered to carry identity cards with them. My father had wanted so badly for his Gentile friends to accept him and to be admitted to one of their prestigious clubs, but now he was forced to carry around a card stamped with a large red letter "J" and branded as a Jew. Then, this month, the Nazis ordered me and my parents to turn in our passports, and these were stamped with a big red "J" as well. We could not hide our Jewish identities.

Why would my parents want me to come home?

The big bay window in back of Mother Superior looked out on a cobblestone alleyway, and light streamed in through the panes as she said, "Rosemarie, your parents are no longer able to send money out of the country, so they cannot pay your tuition."

"So, I must go?" I asked. It was what I wanted and wished, for I had not been back to Germany since the summer of 1936, six months after Margrit married Walter, the son of a local tailor. Those four weeks were the last ones our family spent together. I remembered the velvety sand on the beach at the North Sea and the words from my father's poem: *Those beautiful days at the beach. Only too quickly passed.*

"Rosemarie," Mother Superior said, cutting into my thoughts. "You do not have to go, you know. Even if your parents cannot pay your tuition, you can stay here. You are an excellent student, and I would be pleased to have you continue."

"But the tuition?"

"We have helped other students before."

"That is very kind of you, Mother Superior, but my parents would not allow me to accept charity."

"Rosemarie, your parents are very proud people, but you can stay on with us if you'd like. You are a thoughtful, kind, and respectful young woman and you have been a joy to have here at school. We don't want to lose you."

"That is very kind of you, Mother, but…"

"I don't think that it is really the charity that is bothering you, Rosemarie, is it? Are you homesick?"

Mother Superior smiled, sensing my thoughts. "As much as I would love to have you stay on with us, Rosemarie, it is easy for me to understand your feelings. You must return home then." No sooner had she said that than worry creased her brow. Yes, she had forgotten something and we both knew it.

"What am I saying. It is nearly impossible for Jews to return to Germany right now."

I nodded and Mother Superior took a deep breath. "Yes, the

9

Nazis do not want their Jewish citizens to return home," she said, leaning across her desk and smiling, "but, they do not appear to have *anything* against nuns."

The following morning, I stood in Mother Superior's dressing room with Sister Marlena at our side, and Sister Marlena pressed three fingers to her lips to stifle herself from laughing. "Oh, come now, Sister Marlena!" Mother Superior said, smoothing out the wrinkles of my dress. "This is not the first time you have dressed a novitiate in a habit!"

"But Mother, this is the first time that I have dressed a Jew!"

Mother Superior nodded, a smile rippling across her chin. "Why yes, Sister, that is a novelty!" They both stood back and admired me, as if I was a statue they had chiseled out of stone.

I studied my own reflection in the mahogany mirror, feeling like an old woman instead of a 17-year-old girl. My blond braids were pinned up on my head, and golden curls strayed from under my hat. Wearing this habit, no one would ever suspect that I was a Jew.

"Rosemarie," Mother Superior said with a twinkle in her eyes. "Our convent is open if you ever choose to join our order. I could ask for no finer nun, right Marlena?"

Two fingers on Marlena's right hand crossed behind her back. "Oh yes, Mother! Rosemarie would be a nun for the ages! Like one we've never seen!"

Mother Superior hugged me tightly as I left the following morning. "When you pass through the waters, I will be with you....."

"Auf Wiedersehen, Mother," I said when she finished her Bible verse, and I nearly tripped over the hem of my habit as I walked out the main door and thanked her.

"Auf Wiedersehen, Rosemarie," Mother Superior said. "You shall not be alone, for my prayers will reach you wherever you are."

I boarded a train for Germany, and as the train neared the Swiss station of Basel, on the German border, I felt my stomach cramp. Would the Nazis ask for my passport?

Mother Superior had told me not to show it, because you could only imagine the questions that would arise when customs officials saw that big red "J." A Jew dressed up as a nun?

Mother Superior told me to pretend that I'd forgotten my passport back at the abbey, but my heart pounded as the custom's official walked down the aisle of my car and said, "Passports, please!" One by one, riders reached up to hand them to him. When the border guard reached the seat in front of me, I was sitting on my hands to hide the fact that they were shaking.

"Guten Abend, Schwester!" the border guard said, smiling down at me. He was a short man with a big girth protruding out of his gray uniform and a sandy-colored beard on his chin.

"Abend," I said, wondering whether to tell him the story Mother Superior told me, or to invent a new one of my own. Before I could decide, though, the customs official placed his hand on the back of my seat and continued down the aisle, shouting "Passports!" My heart hammered against my chest as the officer moved on, leaving me alone. My hands still trembled as the train rolled home through the Black Forest stations, especially after passing a group of brown shirts on one platform shouting "To hell with the Jews!"

I'd sent Dr. Molser a polite letter and told him how old I was. I didn't think he'd want to continue writing me. To my surprise, he wrote me right back, and I opened up my purse to finger the thin tissue paper.

15 October 1938

Most esteemed, gracious Fraulein Rosemarie,

Thank you for confirming what Mr. Guttentag told me – that you have struggled abroad under utterly new and quite distinct conditions from the homeland and have mastered them. It has been a difficult beginning for you, who are so young.

My dear gracious Fraulein, nowadays it takes such courage to live. When I moved to the jungle nine months ago, people made faces as if I went to my own funeral! And yet I wanted to preserve my freedom, and I was never so happy in my whole life as I am now. It is a wonderful feeling to have one's fate in one's hands and to build upon it.

Please be so kind as to write openly about yourself. Write and tell me everything that moves you, and what you would like to do with your life.

I will do the same. We want to start off with openness and confidence right from the beginning.

Herbert Molser

I reread Dr. Molser's letter as the train passed the angry brown shirts, and I couldn't stop. I would stare out the windows and then back at his typewritten words. Somewhere in an exotic land, there was a man who was just as lonely as I was. He was bold, and he had taken fate into his own hands. As I smoothed out the wrinkles on the skirt of my nun's habit, I realized that I had done the same, and that I couldn't wait to tell him.

Gert Freudenberg (center)

GERT LIVED IN a four-story apartment building with arched windows and spirals on the rooftops, and I called him on the telephone as soon as I could. I tried on every dress I had in my closet, eyeing myself in the mirror before choosing the one that looked best. Yet Gert didn't seem to notice or care how I looked. He pulled away seconds after we hugged, saying we didn't have much time.

"Time? What are you talking about? I just got home from school," I said disappointedly, "and I don't have to go back. We have the whole day and the whole week or until whenever I figure out what to do."

Then Gert explained that he didn't mean anything about us. He was talking about Suzi, our friend from grade school who had been writing me in Switzerland. Didn't Suzi tell me? The Nazis ordered her family to go to the train station tomorrow and return to Poland.

Suzi lived on the other side of town where the poor Orthodox Jews from Poland lived, in a plain apartment building with crumbling cement and cracked paint. I lived in a three-story beige mansion with red bricks skirting around the first floor and wisteria cascading down from above. There were stained glass windows arched above the front door of my house, eight tall peaks, a couple of chimneys, and windows of every shape and size. In the spring, the wisteria blossomed into breathtaking clusters of blue, white, pink and purple flowers.

At Suzi's apartment building, babies cried in the hallways and stray gray cats brushed against your ankles, cats so skinny their ribs showed.

"Gert, where will they go?" I asked.

"To a little town on the border," Gert said grimly.

The border along East Prussia was nothing but empty fields. It was poor and barren, and the Polish people were not very hospitable to Jews. Suzi had told me about the pogroms she saw, the scary nights when she and her family hid in the cellar because peasants were galloping around on their horses, slaughtering Jews. If things were bad for Jews in Germany, they were even worse in Poland. At least in Germany, Jews felt a little safer because they were more assimilated and accepted, but in Poland they were never welcomed and it was very difficult to earn a living.

"There are rumors that the Polish Jews being booted out of Germany have no place to go once their train stops at the border," Gert said as he picked up a shopping bag filled with blankets in his living room. "The S.S. herded them out of the train and threatened to shoot them if they didn't run fast enough into the Polish fields. It was often the middle of the night when the Jews arrived, and they spread out blankets and slept on the frozen fields."

14

It was the beginning of November, and already frost was settling on the grass each morning.

"Rosemarie, we've got to help Suzi and quickly. We need to gather as many coats and blankets as we can find, and pack bags with bread, cheese and salami. We only have until the morning."

The railroad station in Bochum the next morning was even more disturbing to me than the one I passed in the Black Forest. The platform was teeming with people, including S.S. officers dressed in black coats with one hand on their guns.

One grandmother with a maroon babushka on her head held a little boy in her arms who clung to her neck and cried, "Oma, home!" Mothers held pillow cases full of clothes or dishes in one arm, and balanced their babies in the other. Meantime, babies wailed and toddlers tugged at their parents' coats, begging to be lifted up and held like their younger brothers or sisters. Parents tried to quiet them, but their eyes looked haunted with fear.

Three generations of families clung to each other on the platform. A little girl in dark braids held her doll next to her chest and buried her lips in its hair, staring somewhere into the distance. I tore my eyes off the young girl on the platform and searched the faces for Suzi. "We'll never find her," I said to Gert.

"We've got to."

I walked along the tracks, with one eye on the oncoming trains and the other scanning every face until finally I found Suzi. I hadn't seen her in two years, and she was taller and thinner now, with a pale gaunt face beneath her blond bangs. Like many other Polish Jews, Suzi was fair and blond.

"Rosemarie!" Suzi gasped upon seeing me.

"Take this!" I said, running along the track and handing her my bag.

"It's for your trip!" Gert said, catching his breath. "We gathered everything we could!"

"God bless you that you did this for us," said Suzi's mother, looking down at us from the platform, her eyes moistening.

"Thank you!" Suzi said." I've missed you so much in Switzerland and I'll write you as soon as I can!"

I could see the headlights of the oncoming train in the distance now. It was chugging closer and blowing its horn. Gert and I scurried across the rails and safely onto the grass and then watched silently as the Polish Jews crammed into the open cars. The Nazis herded them in, bashing anyone on the head with their guns if they didn't move fast enough. I could feel my teeth bite my lower lip as the train doors shut and the wheels screeched forward.

We walked quietly along the sidewalk out of town and soon reached Father's old office. It wasn't far from the Bochum railroad station, and there was a new name painted on the window in yellow letters. Mueller & Mueller. The name Julius Marienthal was nowhere to be seen. Gert stopped and looked at me quizzically.

"He can't call himself a lawyer anymore. Just a legal assistant," I said, with a helpless shrug of my shoulders. Father had been a great lawyer, arguing cases before the German Supreme Court, and he had been respected throughout the country by Jew and Gentile alike. Now the Nazis would not allow Father to practice law anymore.

Gert looked around at the downtown office buildings with their ornate carved balustrades. "So what is he doing?"

"Working at home," I said quietly.

CHAPTER FOUR

Gertrude and Julius Marienthal

FATHER BARELY ATE anything now, no matter what my mother cooked.

"Eat!" my mother pleaded that evening, nudging a plate of food closer to Vati, but Father slid it back with his knuckles.

"Gertrude, I can't," Father said listlessly, and he rested his hand on his belly. Father used to love a good meal and a glass of wine, and he'd put on weight before I'd left for Switzerland. It had been difficult to button his beautiful jackets back then, and now a similar jacket hung limply on Father. Something was wrong with Vati, and he could stomach only a bit of bland tea. Even with that, he could only take a few sips at a time.

Mother called Father's personal physician, Dr. Schlossman, and Dr. Schlossman said it was time to run some tests. So we accompanied Father to Augusta Krankenhous – the hospital - for tests the following day.

Vati was the most precious person in the world to me. Ever

17

since I could remember, I woke up on my birthday to see my father wheeling in a special white cart piled high with presents and a cake baked especially for me. Father would lead our housekeeper, cook and nanny in singing Happy Birthday, and my mother, Margrit and Heidi would join in. There would also be a reading of our birthday poem, which Father had written especially for us.

Hail, Margrit!

Or, Long life to Rosemarie!

The cook would ask us what we'd like for dinner, and I could choose anything I wanted. Much to Heidi's dismay, I usually asked for pea soup.

I couldn't even think of soup the morning after we admitted Father to the hospital. There was an emptiness in my stomach that no food could fill. It started when I found Mother in the study in her nightgown. She was sitting in Father's favorite upholstered chair listening to the radio. I heard the names Grynszpan, shot, and more chilling taunts of "Death to the Jews!"

Just when you think that life can't possibly get any worse, it does.

"Mutti, what happened?" I asked, but Mother pressed a finger to her lips, so I tucked myself at her feet and rested my head on her lap and listened. A Jewish boy named Herschel Grynszpan shot a German diplomat in Paris the day before. Herschel was a Polish Jew living in Germany before leaving for Paris to study. His parents remained in Germany, and four weeks ago, the Nazis insisted that they leave because they weren't German citizens. The Nazis then herded them onto a train, bolted the door, and waved the train on to Poland. Now Herschel's family was sleeping out in the fields in a little Polish village. The Poles didn't want to take them in, and the Germans didn't want them back. Herschel's parents and other Polish Jews were starving.

When Herschel heard what happened, he walked into the German Embassy in Paris and asked to speak to the German ambassador's secretary on the pretense that he had a letter he wanted to give him. A clerk walked Herschel down the hall and pretended to introduce him to the ambassador, but the man Herschel met wasn't the ambassador. It was Ernst vom Rath, a German diplomat serving in Paris. Vom Rath was reading the morning mail and didn't even look up to acknowledge Herschel when Herschel whipped out a gun and shot him five times.

The Nazis were screaming on the radio that every Jew on earth would pay.

At 9 a.m., the phone rang, and Mutti answered it with a nervous, "Guten Tag!" My mother and I were both relieved that it was Margrit and not the hospital telling us that Father had taken a turn for the worse.

Margrit lived about ten minutes away from us in an apartment with her husband Walter and their son Peter. Peter was an adorable 2-year-old, a sweet little tow head with tiny teeth who always smiled. Walter and his mother owned a tailor shop, but the Nazi boycott of Jewish stores had hurt their business, because customers who had smiled and chatted with them for years suddenly began walking past the shop window, carrying their suits and dresses into other shops. The cash register held fewer and fewer bills and coins, and now Margrit called to tell us that she and Walter were riding the train to Cologne that morning to gather up all the papers they needed to emigrate.

Margrit asked to speak to me and said, "Rosemarie, I hope you won't mind, but I left your phone number with the nanny in case she needs help with Peter."

"Of course!" I said. I loved to play with Peter, and welcomed any distraction from worrying about Father, the killing in Paris, or about Suzi. It had been a week and I hadn't heard from her.

A sense of doom lurked around us as Mother and I sidestepped the puddles on our way to visit Father in the hospital on the ninth of November.

"Mutti, is that thunder?" I asked as we turned the corner onto Bergstrasse, the street that led to Augusta Krankenhaus, but it was not thunder. It was the sound of boots, brown leather boots clapping against the wet pavement. There were hundreds of pairs on Bergstrasse, a squadron of Storm Troopers, five abreast. They were marching stiffly down the middle of the main street in Bochum, legs up and down in unison and faces grim under their brown caps. The swastikas on their arms swung up and down as they marched.

I shrunk against the wall while Mother's eyes skirted nervously down the seemingly endless line. What were the soldiers doing here? I had only seen that many soldiers once before, and that was on Hitler's visit to Bochum when I was 12. It was before he was elected, and he and his henchmen looked sinister, even back then. "Sieg Heil! Sieg Heil!" the men cried as searchlights beamed down on them from the windows that night.

Now a German shepherd was growling at me, baring its fangs. A Nazi officer jerked it away. "They're not Jews, you stupid beast," the officer said. How grateful I was to escape into the hospital lobby.

Outside, the soldiers began singing. *"Yes, when the Jewish blood splashes from the knives, things will go twice as well."*

"Just get rid of Hitler," Father said up in his hospital room, "and all these rats will go back in the gutter. They'll have to get jobs, and they'll be too busy working to riot."

I didn't argue. Father wasn't feeling well, and he was growing more impatient at the same time. He hated lying around in a hospital bed.

"All right, all right," Dr. Schlossman said, greeting Father on his morning rounds. "So you're in a hurry to get home and leave us. Well, seeing as I can find nothing wrong with you – other than impatience – I will discharge you tomorrow morning. Then you will be free to go home. I'm still not sure what's wrong with you, but we'll keep on running tests."

Father was thrilled. Mother and I stayed with him all that afternoon, as the trampling of boots in the street subsided.

On the way home that night, the drizzly streets were deserted except for a few Storm Troopers. Gone were the squadrons of soldiers we'd seen earlier, and in their place stood a few soldiers guarding a couple of store fronts. There were new signs on the Jewish shops. "Kauft nicht bei Juden!" Don't buy from Jews.

Crystal pointed out those same four words on the door to the butcher shop as we walked home from school with Doris a few years ago. We had just gotten off the bus, and were about to enter the hat shop that Doris's parents owned, which was right next door to the butcher.

There was a knot in my throat, and I couldn't take my eyes off those hateful words. "Come," Crystal said, wrapping her arm around me protectively. "My father's angry and is going to tell his group about them. Father wants to get rid of all those hostile signs."

"They're terrible. Terrible," said Doris, with a comforting hand on my shoulder. "I don't understand how people can be that mean."

Now, on this November day, Mutti yanked me forward so I couldn't gawk. "You're just inviting trouble. Keep moving," she hissed.

At a coffee shop, three Storm Troopers huddled in the doorway. One took a breath from his cigarette and then snuffed out the butt with his boot. I heard words I'd never heard before. Round up the Jews.

Back home, Mother didn't even bother taking off her rain coat. Without a word, she hurried up to Father's study and turned on the radio. Thank goodness my parents hadn't yet rented out the second floor of our house to make money, and we still had use of the floor. Herschel wailed. Vom Rath had died in the hospital, and Herschel was appealing for mercy. *"It's not a crime to be a Jew. I have a right to live."*

I ran up to my bedroom, with its pale blue wall paper and painted white clouds. It was the room I used to share with Heidi before I went to school in Switzerland and she went to school in Berlin. I was collecting all of Dr. Molser's letters and they were hidden in a fabric-covered box in the room. I pulled out the latest one.

6 November 1938

Dear Rosemarie,

The events in Paris are frightening for Jews everywhere. You are such a courageous little girl to cross the border back into Germany, and I wish that I could protect you, who are so young, and help.

I also wish there was more that I could do to help rescue your friend Suzi. Thank you for sharing the sad scene on the railroad tracks with me. You have a very sensitive, caring nature, and you did what you could for your friend, and for that I am sure she is very grateful. I hope that your friend Suzi and her family have some kind relatives who can help them and take them in. It is what they need until they can make arrangements to move on.

Just like you and your good friend Suzi, we all must move on. It was a sad day for me on April 15, 1933 when the Nazis made me leave the hospital where I worked. Luckily I found another medical internship, and soon I got the opportunity to work here. And, I really love it here, not only out of the feeling that I earn my daily bread, but I love the virgin forests and the freedom. Still, the battle continues for both me and you. In my case, I have exchanged one slap in the face for another. Here I am discriminated against for being German, and it is a struggle to earn clients' trust while the Fuhrer is threatening to take over all of Europe. When I have unpleasant disputes, though, I now flee in my thoughts to you.

Soldier on, little girl, and hold your chin high. Perhaps one day I could entice you to make the journey to Africa and taste the freedom that I have.

Herbert

My BEAUTIFUL HOUSE seemed big and eerie tonight. There were too many windows and not enough Hawthorne trees to hide it from the road. I closed the shutters and drew all the drapes to make the house feel cozy again, because it didn't, not with Father gone and the rain pattering and the creepy feeling I had from seeing all those brown shirts and swastikas in the street.

When I was younger, I was never alone. There were parties and servants and my nanny, Sister Ann, at my side. Our housekeeper, Martine, would be dusting my mother's dark mahogany hutch in the dining room, or picking up glasses in the music room. The cook, meantime, would be in the kitchen, chopping onions and scooping them up for the pot on the stove. Now everyone was gone except Mother, me, and the grandfather clock ticking in the hall.

I tried to keep Mother company by reading on the sofa in

Father's study. Mother sat on the other end of the sofa with a hardcover book in her own hand, but her eyes stared out vacantly. Nothing seemed right.

"Where is Margrit?" Mother exclaimed, shaking her cupped hands. "Why isn't she back by now? Ach, I don't have a good feeling about tonight."

When the phone rang on Father's desk, Mother leaped off the sofa and plucked the receiver off its cradle. "Guten Abend. Guten Abend!" she cried.

I looked up from the sofa and closed my book with a hand inside to keep my place. I hoped it was Margrit and not the hospital telling us some bad news.

"Oh, Margrit, I'm so relieved that you called," I heard Mother say, and then her eyebrows burrowed inward and her voice grew grave.

"Margrit, don't leave that house! Send the nanny home and lock the door!"

More silence, while Mother listened. This time, Mutti changed her mind. "Margrit, get over here now before it's too late, and hurry!"

When Mother hung up the phone, she crumpled onto the sofa and closed her eyes. "Mein Gott," she cried. "Mein Gott!"

I bolted up, sending my book crashing to the floor. "Mutti, what's wrong?"

"It's starting!" Mother cried. "The Nazis are retaliating right now. There are hordes of hoodlums, running wild in the street! They're ransacking the Jewish stores in Cologne. Margrit and Walter saw everything when they were there. Windows smashed. Shops looted. Shelves emptied in minutes. If someone tried to stop the thieves, the thugs hit them. Life means nothing anymore."

I was silent. I felt my hand begin to shake, and I placed it under my hip.

"So Margrit and Walter pretended they weren't Jewish, and they ran and caught the train. But when they got home, the nanny was frantic. The S.S. must have known Margrit and Walter were Jewish and raided their home. While the nanny guarded Peter, the Storm Troopers looted the apartment and stole all Margrit's jewelry and silver. Luckily, the S.S. left the nanny and Peter alone."

Mother clasped her fingers together. "Oh, if only your father was here! He would know what to do! He would find a way to protect us!"

"Mutti, calm down…" I said, trying to quell my shaky hand.

"I can't! You don't understand how serious things are now. Mein Gott, it's too frightening. I don't know whether to stay up or go to sleep!"

"Go to bed! You'll drive yourself crazy. I'll wait up for Margrit and Walter."

Father was gone and Mother was beside herself. Someone needed to rise up and take charge, and yet, I could not stop shaking or shivering while Mother undressed for bed. I walked around the empty rooms and stared. Would the Nazis stick to the stores in Cologne?

"Rosemarie, I can't sleep," Mother said about twenty minutes later, appearing in the doorway to the dining room in her nightgown and with her hair askew. "I haven't slept without your father in thirty years. Will you sleep in my room tonight?"

Though I had been an independent teenager in boarding school for two years, I was almost relieved Mother asked. It was a frightening night for both of us and of course I said I would.

I heard an eerie howl outside in the street as I dressed for bed. It sounded like a cat with its tail caught in a door or a dog yelping in pain, but there were too many goose bumps on my arms for me to go outside and see what it was. I wanted Gert, and I walked into the hall to call him, but the phone rang again. This time it was Mrs. Kaminsky, Walter's mother.

Mrs. Kaminsky lived by herself in an apartment over the tailor shop, and the Nazis had attacked her shop. Up in her apartment, Mrs. Kaminsky heard each smash of glass, bash of wood, and cry for Jewish blood. The Nazis bludgeoned the store.

Mother told Mrs. Kaminsky to get out of the apartment right away and into a taxi. She was to come and stay with us. Then Mutti called Heidi at school in Berlin, to make sure she was all right.

"I'm getting dressed," Mother said defiantly, pinning a strand of hair back. "I'm going to be ready if anyone dares come into our home!"

The Nazis wouldn't come for us…would they?

The door bell buzzed like shrieking piano keys, and Margrit and Walter couldn't squeeze past me fast enough. Margrit was clutching Peter, who was dressed in a woolen toggle jacket. His cheeks looked like he'd been clawing at them, because they were raw and red.

No sooner did we lock the door than there was another anxious rap. It was Mrs. Kaminsky, dressed in a long flannel nightgown and slippers. She was wearing one of those granny gowns that hid any shape within. Drops of blood were splattered on her nightgown like polka dots.

"Mutti! What happened!" Walter cried.

"Oy Gott!" Mrs. Kaminsky said, leaning against Walter's chest. "They broke in before I could escape! They stormed past me with bats and poles and started smashing everything. Everything! They were teenagers, and they called me names! I pleaded with them to leave, that I was only a widow, but they ignored me! I saw the window shatter, and fragments of glass cut me. I ran out the door and down the stairs, too frightened to see what they would do next! I forgot my coat, but I was too scared to go back and get it. I thought they would kill me if I got in their way, so I ran down the stairs and didn't look back. I couldn't look at the shop, either! We had that store for twenty-five years, and now it is ruined. Ruined!"

Mrs. Kaminsky leaned against Walter's chest and sobbed. She was frail and thin, and even through her loose gown you could see her chest heave as she cried.

Walter pushed her back gently. "Mutti, are you all right? Are you hurt?"

Head bowed, Mrs. Kaminsky shook her head. I reached out to rub her arm to comfort her, and her skin felt chilled, even through her gown. Though I rubbed my hand up and down her arm to warm her, she wouldn't stop crying.

Walter hugged her again, and I could see that his slender fingers were clenched like claws behind her back. The tailor shop was their livelihood. What would his mother live on now?

The baby jerked his head back and began crying, "He's tired and cold, poor thing," Margrit said, and Mother understood. She swept Peter up into her arms and said "Shh, little one. Oma will put you right to sleep!"

"Thank you. Thank you for letting me come," Mrs. Kaminsky said as we all followed Mother and Peter upstairs. "I called Walter, and when he didn't answer I didn't know where to go. Oy, Gott! What will become of us?"

"The Nazi bastards," Walter fumed. "I can't wait for our exit papers. You couldn't make me stay in this country another week."

Mother and Margrit whisked the baby upstairs to tuck him in bed, and I sat on the sofa in Mother's music room, holding Mrs. Kaminsky's hand while Walter dabbed at her cuts with a wet towel.

Mrs. Kaminsky was still shivering and her teeth chattering. I patted her hand and ran upstairs to rummage around in my closet for something to wrap around her. I'd given the best blankets to Suzi, so I opened all my drawers, looking for something else to keep Mrs. Kaminsky warm. I found an ivory shawl and a scratchy blanket that I had thought wasn't good enough for Suzi, and I pushed the drawer back in, ran downstairs and draped the shawl around Mrs. Kaminsky's shoulders. Then I opened up the blue blanket and spread it across her lap and legs.

Mother said I should go put a kettle on for some tea, and I made a final tuck of the blanket around Mrs. Kaminsky's tiny ankles when the door bell rang. We all froze in the music room, petrified.

"Don't answer it!" Mrs. Kaminsky said, her eyes still moist and red. "It's those hoodlums! They'll destroy your house, too!"

Walter looked at Margrit, Margrit looked at Mutti, and Mutti looked at me. Then we all stared at each other, wondering what to do.

"It's Herr Buchner," a voice called from below. "I need to talk to you!"

Herr Buchner was our next-door neighbor who lived to the right of us with his wife and two sons, Ernst and Heinz. He was an ear, nose and throat doctor, and a good friend of my parents. Herr Buchner would never mean us any harm.

Holding his hat in his hands, Herr Buchner apologized for the intrusion. He knew it was late, but he wanted to warn us to be careful. "Ernst heard from his friends that the Storm Troopers are recruiting all the Hitler Youth. They're to vandalize every Jewish store and home in the country and leave nothing untouched. It's a direct order from Berlin. They were also told to round up the Jewish men and ship them to Dachau or Buchenwald. The Nazis say it's to retaliate for the killing in Paris, but it's more than that. It's the beginning of the final act, to get all of you to leave."

"Oh, they don't have to worry about us!" Walter said, seething. "We're leaving just as soon as our papers come through!"

Margrit leaped up and grabbed Walter's hands. "Walter, if what Herr Buchner says is true, you've got to get out of here! You're in danger!" she said, cupping his hands in hers. " If you get caught and sent to one of those places, I might never see you again! They'll kill you for sure!"

In Germany, we heard rumors about Dachau and Buchenwald. They were jail camps that were built for political prisoners, including social misfits and Jews. The goal at Buchenwald was to work its prisoners to death. The S.S. who ran the camps seemed to be the worst dregs of society, for they ordered men to strip and then whipped them raw. Some men – like the father of Margrit's friend – died from the beatings. These men were cremated and returned to their family in urns.

Margrit rested a hand on Mrs. Kaminsky's shoulder while the elder woman sobbed. Mother picked up the towel that Walter had used to clean his mother's cut and said, "Thank God your father is in the hospital! They wouldn't dare touch him!"

"But what about Walter!" Margrit snapped, jerking her head up to look Mother in the eye. "Walter is NOT in the hospital and we've got to get him out of here!"

Margrit and Walter

CHAPTER SIX

"WE'VE GOT TO DO SOMETHING!" Margrit
exclaimed after Herr Buchner left and Mother slid the deadbolt
across the front door frame and sank into a chair.

What? Walter said he didn't look Jewish and that he should
take the tram to the train station on the other side of town. Maybe
it was safer there, and he could ride the train until the roundup was
over. He could cross the border and be in Switzerland by morning.
Margrit wanted to know what Walter was going to do when the
Swiss border guards asked for his passport.

"Fine," Walter said. "Just walk me to the station and I'll ride the
trains all night." He said he'd hop off before the border, sneak across
the tracks, and climb aboard the other side.

That sounded good to Margrit. "You have got to get out of here.
I'm taking you to that station right now and putting you on the next
train."

Mother thought Walter should hide under a blanket and pretend he was sleeping, just in case the cars were checked for Jews. Mrs. Kaminsky couldn't bear any of this discussion, and began wailing that Walter was all she had. "Mein kind! Mein kind!" she cried.

Margrit pried Mrs. Kaminsky's fingers off her son's neck. "Walter has got to leave," Margrit said gently. "It's for his own safety."

"Please. Don't go!" Mrs. Kaminsky begged. "I'm so frightened!"

"Mutti," Margrit said, her patience ebbing. "It is for the best."

Walter and Margrit left and my mother and I led Mrs. Kaminsky up to Margrit's old bedroom and tried to get her to sleep. Then, we walked upstairs to the third floor to look out on the street. It was the room where my nanny, Sister Ann, used to sleep when I was younger, and the room where I was quarantined with scarlet fever when I was six.

Our house stood on a hill overlooking the city and the surrounding streets of Bochum, and the servants' rooms on the third floor had a panoramic view. The vista was breathtaking. At night, you could see the spotlight on the old theatre, with its caped statues standing guard on either side of the triangular roof. Teapot-like spirals topped the other downtown buildings, and trees edged the promenades and trolley lines.

The third floor was where I'd first prayed as a child, begging God to cure me of scarlet fever so I could play with my friends again. *"God, please watch over Walter and Margrit,"* I whispered.

Mother heard me mumbling and said that Father was right. God was either dead or never alive in the first place and that she'd wasted all those years in the synagogue on Yom Kippur, praying for nothing. Then Mother stopped mid-sentence.

Both of us were watching Walter and Margrit disappear down

the street, but something more shocking caught our eyes. Two cupolas were burning in the midnight skyline, the domes of our synagogue on Wilhelmstrasse. The synagogue Father ignored and the one where my mother and I prayed on Yom Kippur. The place where I had grown friendly with Rabbi David, whom I'd sought after returning from Switzerland.

"Rabbi David, why am I Jewish?" It seemed to be the reason why Inge, Doris and Crystal never called or wanted to see me again.

Rabbi David clasped his hands and looked at me. Then, he rolled his chair forward and rested his elbows on an open book with Hebrew lettering inside. "Rosemarie," said Rabbi David, propping up his chin on his hands. "What is it that is troubling you and what is the real reason you are asking me that question?"

"Because," I said, blinking back tears that at one time never welled on the subject of faith, "I don't understand why my friends hate me, and why being Jewish is the cause of so much shame. You've got to help me understand what sets me apart from other people."

Rabbi David said that what set me apart was my intelligence and goodness, and that my Jewish heritage was not a cause of shame but envy. He also said that my question reminded him of a letter he'd read in a book that had been written over 150 years ago by the German philosopher Moses Mendelssohn. Rabbi David reached up for a book on his shelf, sat back in his chair and read: "'Father ... why do they throw stones at us? What have we done to them? ... They always follow us in the streets and scream at us: `Jews! Jews!' Father, do these people think it is a disgrace to be a Jew? And why does it matter to them?' Ah, I close my eyes, stifle a sigh inwardly, and exclaim: `Poor humanity! You have indeed brought things to a sorry pass!'"

Devilish flames now clawed through the synagogue's gold domes. The entire roof was engulfed, and flames danced in the purplish sky.

"No," I wailed, pressing my nose against the window to get a better look. Not the synagogue and not Rabbi David, for I had come to see that my rabbi was the physical embodiment of everything good. Goodness in man, like compassion, kindness and forgiveness. Goodness in religion such as tolerance and respect for all people and faith, and goodness in Judaism, with the wisdom of King Solomon and the heart and humanity of King David.

Mother and I didn't speak. The grandfather clock broke the silent stillness and chimed. It was 2 a.m. and our hearts were chilled at the sight of the great synagogue burning in the night.

"It is a pogrom," Mother said, when she finally spoke. "This must be what it was like in Poland and Russia. And I thought we were so civilized."

I had never seen a pogrom, for Germany had not had one since Jews were beaten up in seven German cities back in 1879. Now the outside inferno seared my eyes and ghoulish cries ripped into my heart. My eyes were riveted to the window as the flames dipped lower and the once majestic roof of our synagogue sank into embers.

When the clock chimed 4 a.m., Mother and I saw Margrit scurrying down the street, huddled against the wind.

"Thank God you're safe," Mother said as Margit hung up her coat and told us about the drive.

Margrit had dropped Walter off at the station, and she arranged to pick him up at daylight when the madness was through. Then Margrit got a good look at the destruction on the ride home. The synagogue was burning and there were broken storefronts everywhere, but now the streets were deserted.

Mother filled the tea kettle with water, set it on the stove, and turned on the gas. Blue flames licked the bottom of the kettle, boiling the water. Mother poured out three cups of tea, and the three of us then sat at the dining room table, warming our hands on the mugs. Mother yawned, and then I did, and soon all three of us could not hide our tiredness. Mother said we had to stay awake, for it was dangerous not to be alert.

I agreed but counted our blessings.

"We're lucky," I said, and no sooner did I say it than I realized how ridiculous it must sound.

"Lucky?" Margrit exclaimed. "How can you say that? Father is in the hospital and Walter is riding trains to escape a roundup. How can you call that luck?"

"You mustn't think that way, Margrit," Mother said, chiding her. "Walter is very smart and he will find a way to escape. You will pick him up in two hours and everything will be fine."

I was always hungry, and after being awake all night, I looked around for some bread so I could make some toast. Mother reminded us that the downtown bakery delivered fresh rolls each morning. A non-Jewish couple owned the bakery, and the Nazis would never touch them. The rolls were due to be delivered any moment and we could enjoy them with our tea.

"Maybe that's the baker now," I said innocently, as a car drove up to the house.

I ran to look out the window but froze at the sound of angry voices. There were too many voices for that car to be the baker's. I heard men leap out of a car and their boots thud as they hit the pavement. The men sounded drunk and were singing off key. They were singing the Horst Wessel song, the one about blood spurting from knives.

My feet were leaden and my throat was mute.

"Open up, you Jew bitches!" someone barked, and a cacophony of voices whooped with glee. Before we could even unlock the door, an ax swung and wood splintered, chilling us with every blow. A beam of wood bashed the stained glass windows around the front door, and shards of glass shattered across the marble.

Before I could move, boots crunched on the broken glass and stomped up the stairs our way. I came face to face with a defiant young man. He was broad shouldered and stocky, his brows dark and running in a straight line across his forehead. His eyes were menacing and he held a machete in his hand. He slapped the handle against the palm of his other hand as he faced me, teeth clenched.

This man was dressed in normal clothes, and not in the brown uniform of the S.A. or the black of the S.S. Soon there were two men at his side, and then three and four.

Two by two, the army of thugs bounded up the stairs and into the hall to face us. There was a wall of boys and men. I scanned the faces but I couldn't recognize anyone from Bochum. They were unfamiliar faces, red-cheeked and full of hate. I couldn't take my eyes off them or look at my mother or sister.

The stocky man didn't seem to be the ringleader, but an older man did. He scowled at me like a German shepherd, held at bay by his master.

Mother ran upstairs, and I was sure it was to protect Peter and Mrs. Kaminisky. Margrit and I stood there, unsure what to do. Oh yes. We were outnumbered.

The first man looked me and Margrit up and down. His eyes feasted on Margrit, who was wearing a long black lace skirt and white button-down silk blouse. Her blond hair cascaded down around her shoulders, and she was gorgeous, even without any sleep.

"What are two German girls like you doing in a Jewish house?" the man asked.

Two German girls?

CHAPTER SEVEN

Rosemarie (right) and classmates

A FEW YEARS AGO, Inge arrived wearing a new outfit to school. It was a brown pleated skirt with a white blouse and embroidered vest, and obviously Inge had joined the Bund Deutscher Madchen. She was the only one of my friends wearing that outfit that day.

The Bund Deutscher Madchen was the association of German girls, or the Hitler Youth for girls. When Father and I hiked along the Rhine, we saw the Bund Deutscher Madchen on their field trips. Girls raced each other up and down the trails, laughing in the wind. They camped out in the mountains, and marched in parades through town.

I used to take walks through a park across the street from my house with Inge. We would always have something to laugh about – especially our teacher, Herr Wenzel. He was a short, skinny man who never smiled. Inge and I made fun of his thick glasses, and the way his mouth twitched beneath his scrawny mustache when he was angry.

Inge began to avoid me that day she wore the BDM uniform,

which was about the time the words Nur Fur Arier – for Aryans only – appeared on the park bench closest to our house.

Now she stared at the pictures Herr Wenzel, had taped to the front of the room. Pictures of fat bald-headed men clenching bags of money in their hands. Jews.

I couldn't take my eyes off the photographs on the wall that day. One man was dressed in a white sports coat and dark trousers. He walked alongside a shiny convertible carrying a lighted cigar. He was smiling, and you could see his fat cheeks and double chin. I think he was supposed to represent a wealthy Jew, but he didn't look at all like my father, for my father was tall and thin with dark blond hair and blue eyes. Father was handsome - quite different from the men in Herr Wenzel's photographs. Father stayed in shape skiing during the winter and hiking in the warmer weather. On Sunday afternoons, we often rode a train into the mountains and backpacked for hours, spreading out a picnic lunch on the grass along the way.

"Class," Herr Wenzel said, taping up the last picture and turning around to face us that day, "here you see pictures of an abominable race. These are Jews, who are every bit as repulsive as these photographs. Jews are devils, and you should spit on one the moment you see one to ward off any evil spells."

Crystal blinked and then turned to look at me with a sad look in her eyes. She wasn't wearing the BDM uniform. I looked at Doris, whose own eyes were full of concern. While other shop keepers put signs on their windows saying "Don't buy from Jews," Doris' parents didn't.

Others in class covered their mouths to keep from laughing. They knew I was Jewish, and spitting at a Jew seemed rather odd.

Herr Wenzel didn't know that there were any Jews left in my school, because most of my peers had dropped out and enrolled in Jewish schools long ago so they didn't have to say "Heil, Hitler!"

before sitting down in homeroom. But, my parents thought that the school was excellent, that the Hitler mania would soon pass, and that it was better for me to stay where I was.

"How dare you laugh at my lesson!" said Herr Wenzel as my classmates tried to stop giggling and get serious. I was afraid that when they all stopped howling they would let Herr Wenzel know how preposterous he was. After all, I was Jewish and I didn't resemble any of the people in his photographs.

Herr Wenzel walked down the aisle and stood beside my desk. "Rosemarie," he said gently, "please stand up."

I obeyed and stood as Herr Wenzel studied my face and then walked around and examined my profile and the angle of my nose. I was embarrassed standing there with everyone looking at me, but Herr Wenzel seemed quite satisfied about something.

"Class," Herr Wenzel said, "I would like to present the girl who looks most Aryan in our class…. Rosemarie!"

Doris rolled her pencil around and around quietly, while Crystal stared down at her lap. I was not Aryan, I thought, reaching up to wipe the sweat off my temple. But then again, what was an Aryan? Wasn't I descended from a long line of Germans, with a town named in my family's honor 200 years ago?

"Rosemarie," Herr Wenzel said, surprised that I wasn't pleased with his announcement. "You should be proud to be so young and beautiful… and Aryan."

My classmates coughed and choked, much to Herr Wenzel's annoyance. Her Wenzel's mouth twitched and his brows furrowed with anger. "Rosemarie does not deserve this!" he said.

Inge raised her hand. Leave it to bold Inge to set Herr Wenzel straight.

"Inge! What is it?" Herr Wenzel snapped angrily as I grabbed the chance to sit down.

"Herr Wenzel," Inge said, "Rosemarie isn't Aryan. Rosemarie's Jewish!"

Herr Wenzel's face turned the color of white chalk. "Nein," he said, shaking his head. "That's impossible. Rosemarie isn't Jewish. There are no Jews in this class." Wheeling to face me, Herr Wenzel said, "Inge has just insulted you. It isn't true, is it?"

If I denied it, I would be calling Inge a liar, but if I admitted who I was, Herr Wenzel would appear a fool.

"I'm sorry," I said, stammering. "I'm sorry you're new and that you didn't know. I should have stopped you…"

"Nein," Herr Wenzel said, stepping backwards as the other girls nodded.

Herr Wenzel stormed up to the front of the room and ripped all his photos off the wall, and then he tore the pictures into shreds and threw them in the garbage.

"I'm sorry, Herr Wenzel," I said as he pointed his finger at me, eyes bulging with anger. "I'm sorry!" I said, and I meant it. I only wanted to please.

"You are like all the other Jews!" Herr Wenzel cried. "You deceived me! You played along!"

"I didn't mean to," Herr Wenzel," I said, tears falling freely now.

CHAPTER EIGHT

Gertrude Marienthal

"YOU SHOULD BE ASHAMED of yourselves,
working for Jews," the thug said in my house that November.

I had been honest with Herr Wenzel four years ago and couldn't
bring myself to lie even now. I opened my mouth to say I indeed
lived there, but before I could say one word, the destruction began.
The stocky man held his machete like a tennis racket, drew it back
like a two-fisted back hand, and bashed the stately grandfather clock
in the foyer with all his might.

Glass flew everywhere, scattering to every corner of the room.
When the weights of the grandfather clock were exposed, the thug
reached in gently and yanked them out.

He handed the new weapons to his henchmen, who used them
to whip every pane of glass with fury. The glass breakfront on my
mother's beloved dining room hutch – the one that displayed all her
fine crystal and china – was bashed. Delicate, ornately-carved crystal
goblets were clubbed with merciless fury. Dainty cups and saucers

were battered.

A tall blue-and-white Chinese vase was hurled through the dining room window. Now there were jagged, shark-like teeth framing the hole. Cold wind blew in.

There was a bright, colorful oil painting in a golden frame hanging at the end of our dining room. It was a peaceful and pastoral scene, with a Swiss chalet set at the foot of the snow-capped mountains and cascades of flowers blooming in the flower boxes. It was a painting of Southern Germany, of a town like Marienthal where my father's family had lived for hundreds of years.

The painting had been my parents' joy. Now a boy not much older than I was snapped open a pocket knife and sliced away with passion. He tore at the painting from end to end.

Mother was yelling. "Where are my keys? I need my keys!" She appeared to have gone mad, and I couldn't answer her.

My eyes froze on the leader of the group, who found a slender side table and held it up to admire it. Then, he strode over to one of the windows in the dining room and bashed it with the table like the horns of a ram. The glass spewed out and he heaved the table after it. I wanted to protest, but said nothing. I couldn't speak.

The frenzied hatred spilled into Mother's music room. With its yellow fabric wall paper and white lace curtains, this was the brightest room in our house. My mother had been a concert pianist before she got married, and she used to invite concert pianists and opera singers to candle lit dinner parties at our home. I would sit on the balcony with Heidi and my legs dangling through the balustrade, watching my mother or her guests play the piano and sing.

The music room was where we celebrated Christmas each year, despite being Jewish, and hung real white candles on our tree. Father would light the candles on Christmas Eve, and then open the doors to the music room and invite us in. It was just like the opening scene in the Nutcracker on that magical night.

On Christmas, there had been gifts for everyone, including the servants. Our maids came from small mining towns, and my mother bought them table linens and dishes that they could use when they got married. Mother bought everything at Alsberg's, a department store across from my father's old law office, because there was nothing like a gift in a box from Alsberg's. Mother would bring home shopping bags full of presents and lay them out on tables in the music room.

Now a strange, tall man with disheveled gray hair and thick glasses sat down at Mother's Steinway. He laughed and clenched his fingers over the keyboard, looking like Count Dracula on stage. Then, he banged the keys, playing the Horst Wessel song.

Louder, the thugs yelled. To the Furher, they cried!
Comrades... millions, full of hope, look up at the swastika
The day breaks for freedom and for bread.
For the last time the call will now be blown
For the struggle we all stand ready
Soon will fly Hitler flags over every street
Slavery will last only a short time longer.
Flags high, ranks closed
The S.A. marches...

The hoodlums crowded into the doorway of the music room now, laughing at something I couldn't see.

Finally, to my horror, I saw the heads of five brutes. Men walking across the sounding board of my mother's piano. The piano legs groaned under their weight and collapsed. Then I heard more stomping as the men ground my mother's piano into dust. My

43

fairytale childhood was no more than coarse specks of sawdust on the floor.

From downstairs, I heard bottles smashing and glass breaking, and when I walked down to the wine cellar, I saw a couple of thugs drain wine down their throats and hurl the empty bottles across the room.

If Jews were so contemptible, wouldn't their wine be as well? My righteous indignation rose and got the better of my fear. "What are you doing?" I asked. "Aren't you ashamed of drinking Jewish wine?"

A brute smashed me in the face with his fist, and when I fell, he kicked me in the stomach.

I lay there writhing and struggling to breathe as his foot clubbed me a second time. Groaning, but with my eyes wide open, I saw the room where Inge and I played when we were younger. On rainy days, we'd run downstairs to this room and play with my doll house, which was built like a Swiss chalet with a wooden porch and an open back where we could arrange the miniature furniture. There was also a painted black wooden cash register, with brass keys which we punched down when we rang up a sale, forcing a little red drawer to pop open where we could slip in some toy bills.

We played for hours, taking turns with the doll house and play store. When we were done playing, we would run upstairs and chatter all the way across the street to the park, our braids bobbing as we ran.

From down on the floor I watched an older man with a round belly and white hair smash my wooden doll house. My china tea set was next. The old man threw all my books against the walls of the cellar, the ones I had loved to read. As a child, I had spent many afternoons curled up on a chair down here, reading those books and exploring the American frontier. Now, happy memories rained down on me in shards of glass. Red wine splattered everywhere.

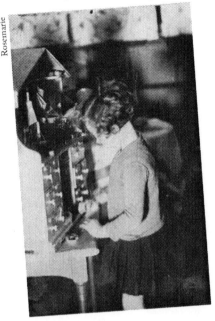

Rosemarie

I grit my teeth and sat up. I had to forget the pain in my stomach and get out of here. My shoes crunched on the glass as I ran upstairs to find Mother. The door to her bedroom was broken, and there were flecks of glass everywhere. Young men hurled her glass perfume bottles out the window, the ones I liked to spray on my wrist at Mother's dressing table.

Out in the hallway, Mother was confronting two men. They wanted to enter Margrit's room, which we had turned into a nursery after Peter was born. Peter was inside, and Mother guarded the door. "If you go in this room, I'll kill you!" she cried.

I grabbed a big piece of glass from the floor and held it up menacingly. I would stab anyone who dared touch Peter. The thugs looked at us and shrugged. Then they turned and moved on. Yet the singing, laughing, and trashing of my house continued.

Finally, there was no window left to break, except in the nursery. Not a mirror was whole. No piece of furniture unscathed. Twenty-three rooms were filled with broken chairs and remnants of our life.

My parents had a painting of the Biblical character Job in the hall, the good man who suffered greatly, the one who lost his possessions and became so ill that he wanted to die. In the painting, Job was scratching the boils on his body, just the way he did in the Bible story. The painting was slashed and the hoodlums gathered. "Time to move on!" one said.

"But what about the upstairs bedroom?" the stocky man asked.

"Nein," another said. "It's just a baby in there, and the Jews will soon be in the furnace if Hitler gets his way."

One by one they filed out, snickering at Margrit.

Margrit tended to the baby, and Mother and I gently picked pieces of glass off the sofa and sat down. All the windows were broken, and we shivered in the cold. I jumped up to find a coat and I saw Mutti's eyes water as she looked around. There were tears running down her face, and it suddenly occurred to me that I had never seen Mother cry. I needed to get some air.

Down in the vestibule, I looked at the once stately front door, now gashed in the center so that you could see outside. Yet there was a more ominous and disturbing sight. A dark green lorry sputtered down the street with an S.S. guard standing on a side step, hanging on. He leaped off and glowered at me. The whites of his eyes were ghastly, and pupils were dark like bullets.

"I'm looking for Dr. Marienthal," he snarled.

A chill ran through me. Packed in the back of the open truck were dozens of men I knew. There were men Opa's age, shivering in the frosty air. Grandfathers of girls and boys I'd grown up with. There were men my father's age, fathers I knew, standing beside their sons. I knew soul after soul in that truck, including Rabbi David. He was standing there, looking at me forlornly, his face raw and bloodied. Gert was there, too.

I ran past the S.S. officer and toward the truck. "What have they done to you!" I cried. "Where are they taking you!"

Gert bowed his forehead and his father shook his head, warning me not to come closer.

The S.S. officer jerked my arm back till I cried out. "Take me to Dr. Marienthal," he sneered. "I've orders to pick him up."

I rubbed my arm and looked up at him and the Iron Cross hanging from a ribbon around his neck. "Dr. Marienthal is …. not …. here… " I stammered truthfully.

The S.S. officer raised his rifle butt. "Don't lie to me!" he hissed. "Bring him at once!"

"He's in a hospital," I said, wiping the offer's spit off my face. "He isn't well."

The S.S. man lunged at me and stared me straight in the eye. "You're lying," he said and then wheeled and motioned for the other soldiers in the truck to get out. "Search the house up and down!" he yelled. "He's probably hiding inside!"

Four uniformed soldiers bounded out of the truck, boots crunching on the glass. They stormed past me, brown coats whipping behind them.

Only one guard remained, standing on the street, with his gun aimed at the back of the truck. "Rosemarie, get back in the house!" Gert cried. "Tell my mother that you saw us and that we're all right!"

I nodded, staggering backwards, as the disappointed soldiers returned to the truck without my father. Gert was my special friend, and now he looked so scared. I could be rounded up next.

CHAPTER NINE

Margrit

THERE WAS A JAGGED HOLE in every window.
Luckily, we had central heat, and we turned up the thermostat as
high as we could. Still, even with the heat on full blast, we needed to
button our jackets.

We bundled up Peter in his coat and hat as well, but he
wouldn't stop coughing. It was a frighteningly deep cough. You
could hear the phlegm rattle around in Peter's chest, and you could
see thick green mucous running from his nose.

Luckily, Walter phoned to say that he was all right. He had
hidden in the bathroom on the train, dodging the porter who
collected tickets. He rode the train all the way south to Stuttgart.
There, he phoned a friend who happened to be a policeman and
knew that the Nazis had a warrant out for Walter's arrest, for they
were intent on rounding up every Jewish man and sending him to a
concentration camp.

Walter was scared. "It's not safe for me to come back to
Bochum," he told Margrit.

Walter said he'd remain in Stuttgart, where people didn't recognize him and he could pretend he wasn't a Jew, so it was up to Margrit to sell off the furniture in their apartment and pack. Then they would meet in Stuttgart and proceed to America.

"It's a good plan," Margrit said, "and thank God you're all right."

Peter was a different story. He was cranky and listless. Margrit hugged him close to her neck and paced back and forth in the nursery, the warmest room in the house. "If we don't do something, Peter's going to die of pneumonia!" she said, and begged Mother to find a doctor.

While Margrit held Peter, Mother began calling all the Jewish doctors she knew, for the Nazis had banned Aryan doctors from caring for Jewish patients. Yet there were very few Jewish doctors left, because most, like Dr. Molser, had moved on to practice in other countries. The ones who stayed behind had been rounded up.

Mother drummed a pencil on a table. "Mutti, please!" Margrit pleaded. "There must be someone! We've got to get Peter to a doctor!"

But who was left?

Mother exhausted her list of Jewish doctors and started calling all the non-Jewish ones. "This is Gertrude Marienthal," she began. "I'm sure you know my husband, Julius. We are in need of a favor."

After explaining the urgency of her call, there was silence while Mother patiently listened, eyes on her lap. Finally, Mother hung up the phone. She dialed a dozen numbers, but as fond as each doctor was of my father, and as grateful as they were for his legal help, everyone was afraid. No one wanted to be sent to a concentration camp. The cost of helping Jews was too dear.

Mother looked out the window at Herr Buchner's house next door and said, "Herr Buchner helped us last night. Maybe he'll help us again with Peter."

"He'll never do it," Margrit said, eyes sweeping downward. "It's broad daylight now, and it's too dangerous."

"He's our only hope," Mother said grimly. "We'll just pretend we're visiting Frau Buchner for tea!"

Margrit wrapped a red scarf around Peter's neck and Mother tied his navy woolen hat under his chin. Then, they all headed next door, and on the way out, Mother gave me last-minute instructions.

"Rosemarie, it's up to you to tell your father what happened. I haven't the heart."

When I closed the front door behind me on my way to the hospital, I was struck by the irony. The front door was gashed. You could reach your arm in from outside and unlock it, so what was the use locking the door, or shutting it? What more damage could someone do? Out in the street, glass was strewn everywhere. It glittered on the pavement as I waded through the debris. There were shards of glass in shops, doorways and streets. There were little slivers and big panes. Shop owners stood speechless, gaping at shattered lives.

A woman cried as she swept glass into a dustbin outside her dress shop and dumped it in the garbage. It was Mrs. Hirschberg, and I had never walked into her dress store without seeing Mr. and Mrs. Hirschberg side by side. Mrs. Hirschberg would bring out dresses to show customers, and then Mr. Hirschberg would tuck a pin here and a pin there for the alternations he would make so that the garments would fit just right. Mr. Hirschberg was always there, with a tape measure wrapped around his neck and a pin cushion strapped to his wrist.

I had never seen Mrs. Hirschberg alone before today.

I hurried across the street so that she wouldn't see me. It wasn't that I didn't care about Mrs. Hirschberg. It was just that I was at a loss for what to say. I had seen Mr. Hirschberg on that lorry this morning, with bloody welts on his forehead.

At the hospital, I had the terrible job of telling Father that his beloved house was in a shambles as he packed up his things for home.

Father listened in disbelief, and then railed away. "Why did the Germans go after me? I'm an important man! I was a war hero and a good German all my life!"

Father's non-Jewish friends – the judges he worked with in Berlin - said that nothing would ever happen to him. "Why didn't my friends tell the thugs to leave us alone?"

"Maybe they did," I said, "and the Nazis didn't care."

Father stared at me blankly. "Didn't … care? Why, I'm not like all those other …. Jews." He bowed his head, and lines deepened on his brow. When we returned home, he wandered from room to room, shoes crackling on the glass.

Father's study was the most painful for him to see. He closed his eyes and hung his head, tottering weakly among the wreckage. I picked up his beloved law books, strewn all over the study with their backs broken. Father knelt before a broken picture and picked it up, gazing at it with glassy eyes. It was a photograph of him dressed in his war uniform. Then he tenderly fingered the Iron Cross smashed at its side.

The Nazis had stomped on both. I watched my father slowly turn the Cross from side to side with his fingers. I watched for a quiet moment and then helped Father stand up, steadying him so he wouldn't fall. He was still weak from being bed-ridden, and it had been months since Father had eaten a good meal. The hair around his ears was whiter than I remembered, and there were a few white tufts on his eyebrows. Father's chin drooped, and his shoulders were hunched. For a moment I thought he would cry.

"I think I'll lie down," Father said hoarsely.

"It's good for you to rest," I told him. I picked up all the law books and placed them back, one by one, on the shelf. Then, Mother and Margrit returned. "It's a good thing that we took Peter to see Herr Buchner because he has pneumonia," Margrit said. "Another day and he could have died."

I held Peter while Margrit spooned out the pink medicine and then comforted him as he gagged. "There, there," I said. "Good boy. A long nap and you'll feel better."

I helped Margrit lay Peter down in his crib, tucking a quilt around him.

That afternoon, I sat on the sofa next to Gert's mother and held her hand. She was weeping, despite every lie I could think of. I told Mrs. Freudenberg that her husband and son had looked well when I'd seen them. Never mind how frightened they both were, because Mrs. Freudenberg didn't need to hear that. Instead, I tried to console her because that was what Gert would want me to do. I wanted to be like a daughter to Mrs. Freudenberg because she didn't have one nor did she have anyone else to look after her.

So I imagined every hopeful possibility I could. That the Nazis wouldn't dare mistreat the men, because many of them were important doctors and judges and there would certainly be repercussions. That the news about the roundups would get out and the world wouldn't stand for this kind of behavior. You couldn't round up free men in a democratic country. Why, it had never happened before in Germany and it couldn't last. The men would be back safe and sound before dark. The Nazis would give everyone a good scare and then stop.

Yet I no longer had any illusions about what the Nazis were

capable of doing, and neither did Mrs. Freudenberg. Why, the Nazis were even demanding that we pay to clean up the mess they had made last night! One billion marks was the rumored fine for "our" abominable crimes.

Mrs. Freudenberg and I sat next to each other on the sofa and did our best to console each other. I patted her hand and she squeezed mine.

Back home, workers carted out the broken glass and furniture and loaded it on a truck outside. Then, they returned and glued in new windows, one by one.

"How did we get someone to help us so quickly?" I asked Mother.

"Vati," she said. Leave it to Father, the once renowned lawyer. He always had connections.

Within a few days, all the windows in our house were replaced, yet there was no word from Rabbi David, Gert, Mr. Freudenberg, or anyone else who had been taken. We didn't know which concentration camp they were being held at, how they were being treated, or when they would be freed. Father sat in his study and called every important man he knew. He tried to work for the men's release, to no avail. If only Father would realize that he, too, was in danger!

"Why don't you move to America with us?" Margrit asked Father. Margrit had sold her dining room set and was advertising the rest of the furniture, preparing to leave Germany with Walter on January 2.

"Margrit," Vati said, "I'm almost 50 years old and I've been a lawyer all my life. A German lawyer, moreover. I don't know anything about American law. All my experience and training would be for nothing. I don't want to go someplace where I'll be a poor immigrant. How would I earn a living?"

"You'll earn a living a lot easier than you would in Buchenwald," I said, gently. "Can't you see the handwriting on the wall, Vati? Hitler wants us out of here. It was quite clear the other night, and if we don't leave, Hitler is going to round you up and send you to a concentration camp just like those other men. Then it won't matter what law you practice or what language you speak. You could end up dead."

Father's eyes fell. I shouldn't have been so blunt, but tonight I needed to be. My father had a wide open view of things when it came to everything except allegiance to his country. Then, he was blind.

Yet moving to America was easier said than done. You couldn't go to America unless you had an affidavit of financial support and a guarantee of employment. The United States didn't want anyone to become a burden on the country, so relatives had to sponsor you.

We had relatives who lived in New York and could sign such an affadavit. My father, in fact, had an uncle who had founded the Hanover Trust Bank in New York and was quite wealthy. We had a sponsor, but then there was the matter of quotas. America would allow in only so many refugees each year, far fewer than the tens of thousands of Jews desperate to leave. You had to put your name on a waiting list in Stuttgart and wait until your number was called.

"At least get a number!" Margrit pleaded. "And then, when it's called, you can decide whether you want to leave or not."

"Ach, I don't feel right about it," Father said.

Mother had another idea. "Why can't we just go to England? It's closer to home and to all of our friends, and Rosemarie can get a job as a maid. Perhaps Father and I can too."

I looked down at my hands. England was a possibility of course. Africa too, for Dr. Molser had been writing me all about his good fortune there. I've been here eight months now, and I have found that I'm happy here, he said. I am the master of my own fate, and I can live a life of honor with my head raised high.

"There is, Africa," I said, testing.

Father was out of his seat in a second. "Never!" he cried.

Mother got up and gently pulled Father back down. "It's disturbing enough that this man writes to you," she said, facing me while settling Father back on the sofa. "We don't know anything about him or his intentions."

My father was back on his feet. "What kind of man writes to a 17-year-old girl!" he railed. "There must be something wrong with him."

"I'll be 18 soon."

Margrit settled Father back on the sofa this time, but she took his side. "Rosemarie, it isn't safe to keep writing this man," she said. "We don't know who he is. A man can say anything he wants in a letter just to get you down there. Then he could kidnap you and try to extort money from us. Who knows what he might do!!"

I turned and looked away. I could tell that Dr. Molser was an honorable man, and that he wouldn't do any of the things Father and Margrit said he would. I excused myself from the room and trudged upstairs, locking the door to my bedroom as quietly as I could.

Inside, I knelt down beside my bed and hunted around for the blue and pink floral box in which I had hidden all his letters. There were about a dozen now, and I read them all again and then tucked them gently back inside and pushed the fabric-covered box under my bed skirt. It was so nice of Dr. Molser to write me so often, and I had the feeling that I could tell him, a stranger, things which I could not tell other people I had known for years.

I had written so many letters back to Dr. Molser that I was

beginning to call him Herbert now, and I gathered another piece of my beige tissue paper stationery.

13 November 1938

Dear Herbert,

It must be lonely down in Africa, but it's lonely here as well. I would like to see a movie, but I can't possibly go there anymore. Not with the Juden Unerwunscht sign displayed. Besides, I have no one to go with to the movies. My non-Jewish friends don't talk to me anymore. I was kicked out of school before going to Switzerland, and not one of my friends called me up to ask how I was or comfort me. No one said a word. And, I started to wonder. Were my friends really my friends? Didn't I mean anything to them? Why was it so horrible to be a Jew?

Now it's getting harder and harder to walk downtown past the broken stores. The windows are empty and the glass has yet to be repaired. It is depressing to see lives broken and despairing, and to see all those Jews Not Wanted signs on the places I once liked to go. Our main department store was not touched on the ninth of November, but that is only because the Jewish owners sold the store and moved to America. It is hard to live in a place when you see that injustice can be done without any punishment and to see your own family talk about moving. Life is hopeless, because the Nazis can do anything they want to us, with no regard for our rights or feelings.

I signed my name and tucked the letter on my dresser until I could sneak off and mail it in the morning. I took one last look at the letter sitting on my bureau, addressed to Dr. Herbert Molser in Stanleyville.

I didn't feel quite as sad.

CHAPTER TEN

THE GESTAPO WORE a black uniform, a red arm band, and a black leather hat embroidered with a skull and cross bones. His eyes were cold, and a chilling portrait of Hitler stared equally hard at me from behind him.

I wasn't supposed to come back to the country from Switzerland. Hitler wanted Jews out of the country for good, which led to a curt letter from the Gestapo ordering me to report to the local office at the Bochum police station and explain.

"You renounced your German citizenship to attend school in Switzerland and returned to this country illegally," the Gestapo said after I sat down.

I gripped the pads on the arms of my chair to steady my nerves, but Hitler's eyes bore right though me and a shiver rippled down my spine. The hairs on the back of my neck stiffened, and a bead of perspiration trickled down my forehead under the hot ceiling lights in the interrogation room. One wrong answer and the Gestapo agent could imprison me this very afternoon. Send me to a concentration camp. There was nothing to stop him.

Gert and his father were home now after their detention in a camp named Sachsenhausen in the middle of Germany. They had been held for six weeks,* but even though they were free now, you would never know it. Eyes and cheeks were sunken, and both Gert and his father were frightened skeletons of what they had been before.

"You know that once you leave the country, you are forbidden to return," the agent said, withdrawing a short dagger from his pants pocket and twisting it back and forth. "And, you returned illegally nevertheless. Is that correct?"

I dug my nails into the chair and nodded, doing my best to look the agent straight in the eye and avoid the skull and crossbones.

"And, since you returned to this country illegally, there must be some repercussions, is that not so?"

I nodded weakly.

"Therefore I will give you six weeks to get out of this country, or…"

I gripped the arm of the chair.

"Or be reeducated in a German concentration camp."

I blinked, for it was the worst of all possible fears. When I had visited Gert yesterday upon his return from Sachsenhausen, he bowed his head and refused to tell me what had happened there.

"I can't talk about it," he said.

And, when Mrs. Freudenberg rushed out with a bowl of steaming hot soup during my afternoon visit, Gert and his father shoved soup into their mouths as if they hadn't eaten anything in weeks.

"My God, what did they do to you?" Mrs. Freudenberg said, reaching out to touch her husband's hands. "Please, talk to me!"

*In 1938, the concentration camps that had been built were used to house political opponents of the Nazi regime. It was only after the Nazis conquered most of Europe that Hitler and his Gestapo chief, Heinrich Himmler, decided to use these camps for the extermination of European Jewry.

Both Mr. Freudenberg and Gert averted her gaze.

"They ordered us not to talk!" Mr. Freudenberg said, his voice rising hysterically. He stared at a picture of his family, smiling in happier times.

Now I had six weeks to avoid being interned at a concentration camp myself, and yet there was no way to get out of Germany in that short a time. How could I get a visa? The waiting list in Stuttgart was in the tens of thousands. It was a couple of years long.

"But sir," I said softly in the interrogation room, "I can't get a visa in six weeks. There is a waiting list, and you have to find a country that will accept you. Next you have to find a relative who will sponsor you, and earn the money to pay the exit tax. How can I do that in six weeks?"

The agent tossed his head back haughtily. "That's not my problem!" he scowled, and pointed to the door with his black-gloved hand. "You have until the first of February to get out of Germany or report here for camp."

I stood up, legs shaking, and walked as steadily as I could out the door. Outside the interrogation room, the waiting room reeked of garlic. Bulbs of garlic hung from the ceiling, just the way my father had said. The Nazis thought that Jews smelled like garlic, and they wanted to make a visit to the Gestapo as unpleasant as possible.

Out in the street, an ankle wobbled and I felt faint. I had no choice but to leave. But in six weeks? And, where could I go?

15 December 1938

Dear Dr. Molser,

It's terrible what the Nazis are doing, rejecting us and casting us off to the ends of the earth. The Nazis want to kick us out, despite all the contributions we've made to Germany throughout the centuries. The Gestapo has asked me to leave, too, and I have no idea what I am going to do.

An old friend of mine was just released from Sachenhausen, but he will never be the same, and now I wonder if I will suffer the same fate. I feel so alone, with no one to talk to besides you. I tried to call one of my sister's friends, Ilse, to see if she wanted to take a walk with me, for I needed someone to talk to. But, Ilse excused herself and said she was busy. I wonder if she really was busy or just afraid to be seen with me.

Life is looking more and more hopeless. The Nazis decreed that Walter and his mother can no longer run the tailor shop because all Jewish factories and stores must be "Aryanized."

Father is helping them sell the shop to a Gentile family so they will have some money to pay the Nazis for cleaning up after the ninth of November. Can you imagine – charging Jews to pay for cleaning up the glass? Father could not even sip his beloved wine last night when he heard that. He buried his forehead in his hand for a long time.

Rosemarie

CHAPTER ELEVEN

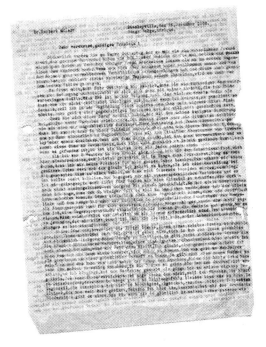

WHEN ALL HOPE seemed lost, along came a letter.

26 December 1938

Most esteemed, gracious Fraulein Rosemarie,

I am sure that you have the same confidence that I have in your uncle, Mr. Guttentag, who is like a fatherly friend to me. This thought might help us both so that my proposal will seem less exotic. My patients keep me busy from morning to evening, and I need somebody to help me. There is a lot of work involved in my medical practice, and I can't perform all the lab tests by myself. My idea is, therefore, to propose a position of "auxiliaire medicale" - medical helper - to you and offer you a six-month work contract which would help you secure a visa. Try to see it as a means to help you leave Germany, because I believe that many people would be very happy if they could do the same.

Because of what's happening to Jews in Germany, we have to create a new country, a new place for ourselves where we feel at home, And right now we have to do that under the equator.

The atmosphere is so calming here, and when one is abroad, he can live a life of honor with his head raised high. Perhaps you can come and work for me and do the same.

With most cordial thoughts,

Herbert Molser

I hurried to hide Herbert's latest letter beneath my bed before my parents could see it, and I was surprised when Uncle Phillip called a few days later from his home in Aachen, a town on the Belgian border. Uncle Phillip sounded jovial.

"Herbert wrote me and asked me if he had been too forward in asking you to come and work for him, and I told him nonsense! There are Jews all over Europe who would leap at the chance to escape! So, are you going? What did you write him?"

I cupped my hand over the phone and whispered, "I would love to go, Uncle Phillip, but Mutti and Vati would never allow it."

"What do you mean they wouldn't allow it! Put them both on the phone at once! Why, I've met this doctor and he's a good man! Let me explain that to your parents."

"I can't. Not right now," I said, still whispering. "They're too upset about Margrit. They're already losing one daughter to America and are hardly eager to give up me, especially to Africa."

"But I thought you needed to get out of the country!"

"I know, Uncle Phillip. But going to both Africa and America are out of the question for me right now."

And after I hung up the phone, Mother pointed out something

in the newspaper.

"Here," Mutti said. "Look at what they're advertising for abroad. Domestic servants. You could be a maid in someone's home, like Leni! It's fairly easy to apply for a permit as a domestic servant, and with that permit you can avoid the long wait for a visa. You could also stay in England for a whole year, until we're able to join you."

I went downtown to pick up the proper form for the permit, and I filled it out and mailed it off to London. A few weeks later, to my utter surprise, England accepted me! The British seemed truly desperate for German maids.

Now that I had my working permit, I visited a few British employment agencies to see about a job, but I returned home empty handed. I had never swept a floor, made a bed, or dusted a table in my life.

"So you don't have any experience?" my mother joked. "Well, we'll make it up!" And, Mother and I sat down and concocted an unbelievable resume. Why, Rosemarie Marienthal could cook, iron and clean like a demon!

The resume worked, for I was soon hired by a British couple named Mr. and Mrs. Bathhurst for the glorious pay of four pounds a month. It was a mixed blessing, though, to leave my parents and take on the unknown.

"It's so far away," Mutti said. Walter had already fled to London as soon as he received his visa, and now he was waiting for Margrit and Peter to join in England, where they would all sail to America. "Margrit will be gone, and you'll be gone, and Vati and I will have no one left. To be separated from you all will be terrible. It will be so hard for Vati and me to endure."

"Then I won't go," I said, reaching for the letter that said I'd been hired.

Mother gripped the piece of paper tightly, out of my reach. "Ach," she said. "What good is it to complain? We must get used to this and build a new life."

Peter was screaming at the train station the day after New Year's. Margrit was wearing a beautiful navy camel hair coat that fell to her ankles, and she handed Peter to Father while awaiting the train to the Hook of Holland harbor in North Holland, where she and Peter would catch a ferry to London.

"Opa, Opa!" Peter wailed over and over again, clinging to my father's neck. Father closed his eyes and hugged Peter close. "There, there," he said. "Opa will come and see you soon."

Who knew when we would see each other again, though, given all the frightening events in Germany? Hitler was making weapons, outfitting soldiers, and massing troops on our borders.

My mother's eyes were moist. "Stay well, my dearest," she said to Margrit, wiping the corner of her eye with her finger. "Soon we will be together only through letters, and we can only express in letters what we feel in our hearts."

Margrit wrapped her arms around Mutti and pressed her head to her shoulder. " I will send for you as soon as I can. Walter and I will work and earn the money you need to go."

"Let us hope that God gives us the strength to find our way to each other in health," said Mutti, as she straightened up from the embrace. "We will all be together again when there is peace."

My parents and I stood on the platform and waved, watching little Peter lean out the window and cry, reaching for Oma and Opa. That night, I pulled out a piece of stationery and began writing to Herbert:

2 January 1939

Dear Herbert,

Today I had to say good-bye to my sister Margrit, and I'm terribly unhappy about it. Margrit is on her way to America, and soon it will be my turn to say good bye to my parents. Thank you for your kind offer to come and work for you in Africa, but I'm going to England next month. I can't think only of myself, and it is important that I go to England and help my sister Heidi acquire a working permit there. She's only 16.

In any case, I think it would be best if I worked in England for a while and we continued writing to each other. I don't really know you that well.

To say good-bye to all that is familiar to me is so hard. I love my parents dearly and the thought of us being separated is very painful. Sure emigration has the flavor of adventure, but life with my parents is comforting and nurturing. I had an enchanted, beautiful childhood and now I am faced with the certainty that it's all over and that I have to leave all that is dear to me. But, I will do everything to have courage and trust my lucky star!

Rosemarie

6 January 1939

Dear Rosemarie,

What you write to me about saying farewell to your parents is very understandable because I have just gone through it myself. I love my parents more than anything. They were so brave when I said good-bye, and I lost my composure when I was alone with my father at the last minute. My mother wisely decided to look for a taxi, and I told my father: "Thank you for all that you did for me in life. I promise you that you will soon get good news from me." They did not have to wait long, and presently my parents live through the letters and money which I can send them. I was able to send them my first bank note that I earned, and it was comforting to them given the circumstances in Germany.

It would be shameful if one were to separate from one's parents lightheartedly. But what use would you be to your parents if you stayed with them? Parents always want to realize in their children the fulfillment of their wishes, and this is nowadays impossible at home.

Herbert

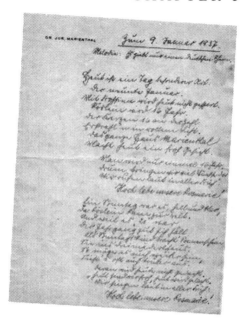

ONE WEEK LATER, my parents wheeled in the white cart as they always did, but there were only two presents on the cart this year - a new winter coat to keep me warm, and a poem from my father.

Today is a very special day
One is just once 18 years old
We present our good wishes
And with full voice at daybreak we proclaim
Long live our Rosemarie!

The time of childhood is over
Now the seriousness of life begins
Stay cheerful and alert and pious and free

See to it that you learn a lot
Keep your mind open for noble things!
Then you can look towards the future with full confidence.

Regrettably there are not many gifts
Since times are hard.
You know we would have liked to give you
Whatever that your heart desires.

We gathered around our dining room table and savored Father's poem again before tasting the cake. My eighteenth birthday was a fleeting boost to our spirits for there were empty chairs where Margrit and Walter once sat. It could be years before we looked across the mahogany table and into each other's loving eyes.

"To be separated from Margrit and Walter is so hard," my mother said as I blew out my candles. "When I have a quiet moment, all I do is look at the pictures from our past. That's all I think about. I'm so filled with longing for what used to be."

"There has to be peace," Father said, reaching across the table and tenderly picking up Mother's hand. "You remember your beloved rose bush? Winter is here, but the roses will bloom again."

Gert was released from Sachsenhausen and scheduled to leave Germany the second week of January. He had decided to take advantage of the Kindertransport, a rescue program sponsored by Great Britain. The country offered to ferry in Jewish children by boat and train and find homes for them with British families.

At 18, I was past the cutoff age, but Gert hadn't yet turned 18 and was still eligible. When I went to say good-bye to Gert the afternoon before his departure, I was pleased to see that he had lost the gaunt look to his face, yet his eyes revealed that his torment had not ended. He was far away from me.

"Gert, what did they do to you at Sachsenhausen? Tell me, please!"

We were sitting in his bedroom, with Gert at his desk and me on his bed, leaning against the wall. "Rosemarie, stop asking me that!" Gert said, twisting angrily in his chair. "Don't you understand? They ordered us not to talk!"

"I know, Gert, but how would the Nazis know? I wouldn't tell on you, so you're safe with me!"

Gert stopped twirling around in his chair and hissed, "No one is safe in this country! They led a man who had squealed out into the courtyard and whipped him in front of us. They said he had told his neighbors about what went on at Sachsenhausen, and this is what they would do to anyone, ANYONE, who dared do the same. They whipped that man the entire night, and ordered us to stand at attention in the cold and watch. Do you understand what it is like to watch a man being beaten to death? I will never forget those screams or his red flesh. Is that what you want me to tell you? Is that what you want to hear?"

"No," I said softly, as my hand began shaking. "No, I was only…trying… to help." When Dr. Molser had seen terrible things in Germany, it had not made him bitter like Gert. Just more determined to get out.

"Rosemarie, things are not the same in this country of ours, nor am I the same," Gert said, turning his head and staring at a corner of the wall. "Maybe it's best that we go our separate ways because I am not the boy you remember. There is a darkness to me that I cannot escape from. It is better that you forget me."

"No, Gert. I could never do that."

"Then promise me this."

"What? Ask me anything, Gert. Anything!"

"Take care of my mother and father until I can send for them."
I gave my word.

16 January 1939
My dear Fraulein Rosemarie,
The arrival of a mail carrier plane is announced here by three siren sounds heard all over the city. And 1 ½ hours later one can find one's mail in the post office box. Today I already passed by a little earlier and, among the half dozens of letters, I first looked for an unusual writing and the post mark of Bochum. It is so nice if one expects something and is not disappointed.

It was wonderful to get your letter. I've read your letter many times and I understand and appreciate all your sadness and longing at leaving Germany. Do not forget that I, as a physician, can also glimpse into people's souls and so I can fully put myself in your position. To create nowadays a new homeland for oneself is a major undertaking. Yet even this black continent is not so dark if one lives here. You can see if you come here yourself that it is absolutely normal here, even though the jungle is at a distance of a few kilometers. Why don't you come after you go to England? You could work for me as a nurse, rather than as someone's servant. And you are far too intelligent and talented to work as someone's housekeeper. Come here and hold that head up high! I promise that I will make the trip worthwhile and treat you with the kindness and respect you deserve.
Herbert

26 January 1939
Dear Herbert:
I understand what you say about living for letters. We are so thankful for our first letter from my sister and her husband from America. The unending separation is hard for all of us, and you don't know how

happy we are to receive a letter from them. Their warm letters dispel the winter chill. All we want is to be together again.

I had to send my luggage to the Foreign Currency Office so that they could check it. First I had to suffer the embarrassment of packing in front of three customs officers who watched to make sure that I didn't hide any silver or jewelry inside my clothing. They were very sympathetic to my embarrassment, but still they watched. My father insisted that I pack everything I could because we don't know when they will be able to send me anything new. Finally, I was done and the customs officers sealed my two suitcases and carted them off. Now I must wait for the suitcases to be returned to me after yet another inspection.

I am so impatient and restless, and I have to learn to wait without losing my patience and getting on the nerves of the people around me. I'm trying to learn a little cooking so that my boss won't be too upset when I come to work.

As for coming to Africa, I am still very young and do not have much experience with people. I can only accept the risk of working for you if you firmly promise me that, if we try it out together, you will grant me as much time as I need to get to know you. The distance and the climate in the Congo do not scare me, but the thought of going to a total stranger in strange conditions is very difficult for me. It is not cowardice or mistrust but rather the great fear that I could make you and myself most unhappy.

Rosemarie

2 February 1939

My dear Fraulein Rosemarie,

I found it awfully nice how you confided in me about your doubts. I understand them, too, for you would be placing yourself not only in the hands of a foreign country, but also in the hands of a stranger. You certainly will have the time to get to know me through my letters – who I am and how I think. And it will be totally up to you to make a decision about whether to come here after your stay in England.

I wrote to you how happy I am here. Do share this happiness with me! I have always succeeded in getting along with people I cared about, and because I wish this with all my heart, we will succeed!

Herbert

9 February 1939

Dear Herbert,

My heart was pounding when I opened your letter. I have to tell you honestly that your letters are wonderful and help me to get over the worst. I'm glad you understood, and I'm looking forward to the day when I can come to Africa and we can talk to each other in our mother tongue.

I visited my sister and your parents in Berlin, and your parents were so lovely and kind to me. They showed me your photographs and told me all about what a wonderful son you have been to them. Your parents are so proud of you, and they miss you terribly. It's a shame that they won't leave Germany because I don't think your parents are aware that they will only see you again if they leave Germany. Your mother told me to take good care of you if I ever get to Africa, and I promised her I would. I hugged your parents tightly when I left them, so dear had they become in such a short time. It was a reassuring feeling for both of us to have the opportunity to get to know each other.

If we want to try working together, it goes without saying that I will come with the best of good will and with the greatest energy. However, please do consider each pro and con as I do. We both still have a long life before us and do not want later on to feel sorry about it.

Below is my new address, for I believe that this will be my last greeting to you from Germany. May it bring a bit of our homeland to you since I cannot bring it over to you myself just yet!

Rosemarie

CHAPTER THIRTEEN

THE HOUR OF DEPARTURE CAME. I closed
the black gate and took one last look on my way to the train station,
with my two suitcases resting on the sidewalk. I wanted to say
good bye to every little spot before my trip to England, especially
my home. Perhaps it was a false sentimentality, but that was me. I
would miss this gabled house, although it was not the same without
Margrit and Heidi, and I shuddered every time I remembered what
happened exactly three months ago on the ninth of November.
Still, this house had been my home for 18 years, the place where
my father wheeled in his birthday table, and where Heidi and I had
played.

This wasn't good-bye until school vacation in Switzerland. This might be good-bye for a very long time. "First Margrit and now you," Mother said, sniffing back tears as we walked toward the tram. Her hands were trembling.

Father was trying to hold himself together, and I held his hand, trying not to cry as we boarded the tram at the bottom of the street for the train station. Who knew how things would work out in England? I had a classical education in Latin, Greek and French, but my English was terrible, so how on earth could I manage there? Not only that, but I knew absolutely nothing about housekeeping! I had never swept a floor or turned on a stove, and I didn't know what to do in a kitchen besides eat. I had tried to learn a little cooking the past few weeks, but I was really hopeless.

Still, I was leaving for England just in the nick of time, for Hitler was making frightening speeches, threatening war. And, as my parents and I rode the tram and got off at Kortumstrasse for the train station, we discussed the latest oration. A week and a half ago, Hitler stood in front of the Reichstag and threatened to kill every Jew alive if war broke out between Germany and the West. It was the sixth anniversary of the day Hitler had been elected chancellor. Hitler's chilling words haunted me still. "If the international Jewish financiers ... should again succeed in plunging the nations into a world war, the result will ... be ... the annihilation of the Jewish race throughout Europe."

"I don't want there to be another war," Father said as he held open the door to the train station. "I lost two brothers in the last one, and that was supposed to be the war to end all wars."

"Three," I said quietly, heading inside. "You forgot about Ferdinand." The brother who committed suicide because the war never really ended for him, but still exploded in his mind.

"Yes," said Father pensively, as we stood in front of the ticket counter and purchased our tickets for the train. My parents were going to ride with me to the border and then head on back home. My father believed that Germany was his home, and that no one had the right to tell him that he had to leave.

On the train, I looked at my passport photograph and at the new red J stamped over my name. That red J and the middle name of Sarah which the Nazis had given me made me extra glad to be leaving, for there was no hiding the fact from anyone that I was a Jew.

A well-dressed one, I might add. I was wearing the new coat that my parents had given me for my birthday. Mrs. Hirschberg had cleaned up her shop and opened it for business again after the ninth of November, and my parents had been one of her first customers after the night of destruction. Mrs. Hirschberg was feeling much better after her husband returned home safely from Sachsenhausen, and she made me this beautiful coat with her husband's help. It was a stunning coat with a black fur collar, and it kept me warm whenever the doors on the train opened, for it was long and heavy and swept all the way down to my ankles. I felt like Marlene Dietrich wrapped inside, because it was a luxurious coat just like one the famous German actress would wear.

"Rather overdressed to be a chambermaid, aren't you?" Father chuckled.

That I was. Yet being a chambermaid might be just a stop on the way to Africa. I could work in England as long as I needed to, or until I could earn the money to save my parents. It was important to help them obtain a visa to England, where they could escape Germany and wait safely for an American visa. But after that, I might want to go to the Congo. That was my little secret, and I felt horrible concealing that from them. My parents didn't know that I had no intention of staying in England forever.

"Take this," Father said, handing me an envelope. "There are

20 German marks. Hide them in your coat and don't show them to anyone. I would give you more, but it is against the law for you to take out more than that, so hold onto the money and use it sparingly. Save it for an emergency, and if your job doesn't work out, find Mutti's cousins in England. Maybe they can help you."

That was not likely. My aunt and uncle had not invited me to stay with them, even though they knew I was coming.

"We can call each other from England, right?" I said.

"Yes, but it will be expensive," Father said. "Better to send us a letter and let us know how you're getting along."

The train stopped at the border sooner than we expected, and it was now time to part our ways. "Auf Wiedersehen, Mutti," I said, lips trembling.

I then moved on to Vati. "Auf Wiedersehen," I said. There comes a time when all children had to separate from their parents, and I was no exception. Still, it wasn't easy.

I would miss them both. "We will all be together again soon," said my father bravely, but he wore a smile like an overcoat. It covered up just about everything inside, all his worry and fear of what would become of his daughters and his homeland. Father's health wasn't good, and despite all the tests Dr. Schlossman ran, there was still no explanation for why he felt so sick.

My mother's eyes were filling and she was trembling. Would I ever be able to go back to Germany and see my parents again? None of us knew the answer, and it was like an inscription Herbert had shared with me. He saw it on a war memorial at his school in Berlin. "Be manly and strong," the veterans' memorial said, and I knew Herbert was right. We would all have to be very strong and patient until the time came when we could see each other again.

My parents got off the train to cross over and catch the next one for the return trip to Bochum. I remained on board for the trip through Belgium to the coast and waved. As I did, tears fell down my cheeks. I had grown up in a beautiful home with two wonderful parents who had loved me with all their heart and had given me the finest things that money could buy. We spent so many happy times together – hiking in the country and bicycling along the Rhine. We'd laughed over Father's poems, and sung songs about our homeland.

Now it was over. Our house at No. 11 Parkstrasse was crumbling and I was moving beyond my parents' protection.

My throat was choked up and I could barely swallow as I settled down for the next leg of my trip. The countryside looked stormy because I watched it pass through a haze of tears. A border patrol guard walked past and saw me. He reached into his pocket and pulled out a handkerchief. "Be glad you are leaving little girl," he said, "for I wish it was me."

CHAPTER FOURTEEN

Rosemarie

I BOARDED A BOAT in Antwerp. Out in the English Channel, the boat reared up and plunged downward on one white cap after another, and I became seasick.

Thankfully my coat stayed clean. In Dover where we docked, I saw the white cliffs that I had heard so much about, but my awe at seeing them was snuffed out by the realization that I had to find the train to London and that I didn't speak English very well. I heard the British people speaking English around me, but I only understood a few words here and there.

When the boat docked and I walked down the plank, I tried my best to read the signs around me. I followed the crowd, hoping that they were heading toward the train station.

Luckily, they were. At London's famous Victoria Station,

I swirled around and looked at the crowds of people, hoping to recognize the woman who was expecting me. I had mailed her a picture of me, so that she knew what I looked like, but I had no idea what she looked like and I wondered if, in fact, she did resemble a tall dragon the way I imagined her.

All of a sudden I spotted a stern looking woman holding up a sign that said "Rosemarie Marienthal." She was grey-haired and dowdy, with all the cheer of a damp, drizzly day. Her grey hair was pulled back tightly in a bun, with netting tied around it. She wore a short black coat that looked like it had hung in her closet longer than I had been in existence, and it wasn't any style I could remember. I looked down at my own new coat and felt rather embarrassed, particularly with its rich fur.

Mrs. Bathhurst did not smile when I approached her. Instead, she looked me up and down while barely moving her chin. "Well it's about time you got here," she said. "Quite late, aren't you? And not at all what I had expected."

What did Mrs. Bathhurst say? I smiled as politely as I could, trying to imagine what she said based on the few words I understood. I thought Mrs. Bathhurst was telling me to pick up my suitcases and follow her, which I did.

But, as soon as I picked up my two brown valises, Mrs. Bathhurst turned her back on me and started walking quickly toward the tunnels. Was she abandoning me or was I expected to follow? I had no choice but to follow the back of Mrs. Bathhurst's coat all the way to another train. If Mrs. Bathhurst left me in that train station, I was in trouble. I didn't know much English, had never met my mother's cousins, and I doubted I had enough money to sustain myself for very long in a hotel. In any case, I clearly did not have enough money to return to Germany, even if the border police would let me in. I had slipped back into Germany once, but twice could be the death of me.

There was a parked train on another track with its doors open, and Mrs. Bathhurst slipped inside without turning to beckon me. I settled on the seat next to her, and without a word we were off to High Wycombe. The train swayed along the track and I looked out the window at the city. My new life was unfolding on the tracks and I had absolutely no control over it. Meantime, Mrs. Bathhurst scowled, sniffing every time she turned to look at me.

Mrs. Bathhurst appeared horrified to find me so well dressed. From the looks of my clothing, you would have thought that I was the mistress and Mrs. Bathhurst was the servant. I had pretended to be 28 on my resume, but I surely looked much younger. I was hardly the robust, experienced German housekeeper my mother had advertised on my resume.

I tried to smile when Mrs. Bathhurst glared at me, but it did not soften her look. It was a terrible beginning for both of us.

In about half an hour, I crossed the threshold of a tiny cottage with none of the twentieth century comforts I was used to back home. There was no central heating, and it was colder in the Bathhurst's home than it had been in my house after the ninth of November. There were two stone fire places at either end of the house, and a wooden stove to warm the kitchen. Flecks of mustard-colored paint cracked from the walls and peeled onto the floor.

Mrs. Bathhurst led me up a creaky staircase to meet her husband in his study. He had pudgy cheeks, thick glasses, and a double chin. He wore a torn knit tweed vest and reminded me of Humpty Dumpty.

"So this is the German housefrau we hired," Mr. Bathhurst said. "Rather well dressed isn't she?"

He stared coldly at me over the top of his tortoise shell glasses.

If I was looking for sympathy after leaving my parents, I wasn't going to find it in those steel gray eyes.

"Do you think she can cook?" Mr. Bathhurst said. "A little wiener schnitzel perhaps?"

Mrs. Bathhurst grunted. "She'd better be able to cook and clean or I'm kicking her out in the morning. Whatever did that agency mean when it said she was highly experienced? And she looks rather young."

Mrs. Bathhurst escorted me wordlessly to my room, which was really the size of a closet. It was furnished sparingly with a stiff cot, a narrow black dresser, and tiny wash basin. There was a pool of ice at the bottom of the sink were the water had frozen and could not drain.

That night, I could not undress for bed. I wore every piece of clothing that I did on the train, including my coat.

The next morning, I awoke to find the water in my sink still frozen and to hear an angry rap on my door.

"Get up you lazy bones! Time to go to work! We didn't hire you to sleep, you know!" The dragon had spoken.

With no time to brush my teeth and no time to change my clothes, I threw off my coat, tied on my apron, and opened up the door as quickly as I could. Then, I followed.

First stop, one of the downstairs fireplaces. Mrs. Bathhurst pointed to a messy pile of kindling wood on the side of the sooty hearth and then more wood stacked clumsily outside.

"You are to build a fire every morning no later than 7 o'clock so that it is toasty for my husband and me when we awake. Is that clear?"

I nodded on cue, though I had absolutely no idea how I was going to tend to that fireplace. I had never built a fire before. We had central heat in our house back in Bochum.

Next, Mrs. Bathhurst led me to her bathroom, the lone bathroom in the house, and demonstrated how to turn on the tap water and draw her bath each morning, even though it was something she could have easily handled herself. Her husband snored in the bedroom.

Next Mrs. Bathhurst waddled toward the kitchen and removed a carton of eggs and a pot. Surely I could boil water, couldn't I?

That could be a catastrophe for there was no stove and I had never cooked anything on a hearth. Cooking over a roaring fire seemed so primitive to me, and I had no idea how to boil eggs the way we used to eat them at home, soft boiled with a solid outer shell and a runny yolk.

Mrs. Bathhurst opened a bottle of smoked herring and poured out three tiny fish onto a saucer. Serve herring every morning? Was that what she wanted me to do? Herring smelled ghastly.

Mrs. Bathhurst breathed a heavy sigh of disgust when I looked at her blankly after every torrent of words, understanding only a fraction of what she said. I was to cook without a gas stove, clean without a vacuum cleaner, and tend to Mrs. Bathhurst and her husband without fully understanding her demands and without any of the appliances I had taken for granted back home. The Bathhursts could obviously afford a maid, and enjoyed the power to order me around, and yet they lived sparingly. That night, after an exhausting day hauling in firewood and dusting the furniture, I cried myself to sleep.

The following morning, I leaned over to pick up the newspaper outside on the driveway when I heard a cheery voice in a language I knew well.

"Guten Tag!"

I turned to see a young woman about my age sweeping weeds off a sidewalk next door. The girl wore a white apron under her brown coat, and her long hair was woven neatly in braids. She waved at me and smiled.

"Welcome to England, and it's so good to live next to someone who speaks my language!" she said in German.

I smiled and walked across the yard, feeling exactly the same way. "But how did you know I was German?" I asked.

"Oh, my employer told me! She said that Mr. and Mrs. Bathhurst had hired a German housekeeper, and I couldn't wait to meet you. Kind of like a little gift from home, don't you think?"

"You're German?" I asked.

"No. Close," the girl replied. "Austrian. My name's Greta!"

Greta was a Jewish refugee from Vienna. The boldness with which she introduced herself, and the spunky way she swept the walk made me believe that she was a couple of years older than me. There was a sureness to her speech and gait that I had yet to acquire.

"How did you happen to come here?" I asked.

Greta told me, and it was a story not much different than my own. Her father had owned a jewelry store in downtown Vienna with many loyal customers. That all changed last March when the Nazis swept through Austria. While most Austrians rejoiced at the Anschluss, Greta's father watched the street scenes with trepidation. He had heard Hitler's speeches against Jews.

Sure enough, the Nazis wasted no time barging into his store not long after they arrived. They seized him by the arm and forced him to open his safe with a machine gun pointed at his head. Trembling in his suit, Greta's father turned the lock and watched the Nazi soldiers elbow past him and raid the safe, gleefully stuffing a fortune of diamonds and jewels into their pockets. Soon the safe and display cases were bare. The Nazis added insult to injury when they left, for they painted a sign on the window. "Don't buy from Jews."

"There wasn't anything left to sell," Greta said, shrugging off the end of her story. Now she was working in England and sending all her wages home. It was all her parents had to buy food.

The news from Vienna grew worse by the day. The Jews were to leave their homes and move to a "reservation" in Poland. The same as Suzi, and I'd yet to hear that she was okay. "In any case, they're stalling against going to Poland, but they haven't figured out where else to go."

I looked at my watch and noted that twenty minutes had passed. "I had better go," I said. "My employer will be looking for me and if I don't hurry she'll throw me out in the street."

"You and all the others! Be careful!" Greta cautioned, and then we made a pact to help each other. I promised to clean all Greta's floors and bathrooms, and Greta promised to cook and iron for me. By sharing the work load, we could please our employers and share news from home.

"Rosemarie, where the devil are you?" Mrs. Bathhurst shouted from a brown U-shaped porch outside her bedroom, her nightgown billowing up around her stumpy legs.

"Any monkey business and I'll send you straight back to the Germans, I will!" Mrs. Bathhurst said, waving her fist. Then, she stormed back into the house.

"The dragon has spoken," I chuckled in German, waving good-bye to Greta.

"That woman is a dragon," Greta laughed. "You're right!"

16 February 1939

My dear Rosemarie,

The mail plane didn't arrive today, and that gives me more time to write to you. Maybe you're already in a strange new land and you have to endure the terrible pain to leave your parents and your home. I know it because I went through it myself, and unfortunately we are not spared. But you are such a brave girl and I know you won't let it get the better of you, and through your tears maybe you can smile. You are so courageous and I know you will pack your suitcase with your chin up and smile bravely when you carry it to your new home.

We don't know each other yet, and still our wishes for the future are so identical. You are bothered by injustice, and feel that those who are unkind and unscrupulous must be punished, and that those of integrity should be honored and rewarded. How hard it must be for you to watch what is going on in Europe right now, to see good people suffer because of their faith. I feel that good people do ultimately triumph, and that all good men receive their due reward in time. I only hope that it will not be too long before the Nazis are thwarted in their efforts to rule Europe and that all of us can freely vacation in the spots we once loved in our youth.

I will hope that your new family is treating you well, because you so much deserve that, and I wish that instead of going to England you could come here. Here, I can protect you, and I long to keep you out of harm.

Take care of yourself in England. I am thinking of you always.

Herbert

18 February 1939

My dear Herbert,

Already the second Sunday afternoon here. The days fly swiftly and still each one is terribly long and each minute has to be endured. I am awfully ungrateful when I should thank my destiny that I am out of Germany. And yet still I am in a terrible state.

You are the only person to whom I write this. My letters home are always cheerful since my parents are already so unhappy. You may not believe how dissatisfied I am, first with my work and second with something that is much more important, free time. I can hardly do anything from here to arrange to go to Africa. I have been here two weeks, and Mrs. Bathhurst is still not yet ready to give me a free afternoon. She says that she will in time, and I will need a whole day in order to go to London to arrange for the trip to Africa.

Don't be angry with me if you don't hear from me as often, for you probably won't get very many letters from me. My parents gave me international stamps before I left Germany, but I'm usually too preoccupied to write nowadays. Just remember that I'm going to use all my free time to try and get my parents out of Germany. The difficulty in Germany has been a tough education for both us, but we always have to tell each other that the fight is worthwhile.

Rosemarie

CHAPTER FIFTEEN

Rosemarie

Soon there was new news to share with
Herbert. Mr. Bathhurst had taken sick. He was horribly bloated
and cramped, and Mrs. Bathhurst accused me of poisoning him. I
might have, accidentally, because I was the worst of all cooks, but
Greta had taken over much of my cooking. And, when the doctors
operated on my employer, they found something far worse.

Cancer.

Now Mr. Bathhurst was bedridden. I felt like my job had gone
from bad to worse, from chambermaid to nurse, because I was often
called out of bed in the middle of the night to help Mrs. Bathhurst
change his bed linens. It was a dreadful existence for all of us, but
most of all for my employer. The poor fellow was suffering terribly,

and I only wished for his sake that he would die soon. Better to go to the next world than endure a life of pain in this one.

It was rare that I slept undisturbed anymore. "Wake up, Rosemarie!" Mrs. Bathhurst would say, pounding on my door in the middle of the night. Mrs. Bathhurst gave me a very bad headache, but my angry feelings would dissolve when I saw Mr. Bathhurst looking up at me, groaning because his stomach hurt him so. I could change the sheets and fluff his pillow and try my best to make him comfortable for the rest of the night, and I sensed how Herbert must feel. It must be hard to be a doctor when someone is suffering and you're powerless to fix it.

I couldn't be sympathetic for long, though. "Hurry up! Hurry up!" Mrs. Bathhurst would yell in her nightdress. "Don't stand there feeling sorry for him. Get him cleaned up and get on out of here so I can catch a few winks till dawn!"

I still couldn't understand everything my employer said, although I wasn't stupid enough to miss the urgency in her voice. And I was so tired of fighting the dragon lady that I did my best to just ignore her and keep my spirits up. Nothing was easy in the world, and it was a daily struggle all over. Here, in Germany, and in America. Margrit had been in New York for two months now, and she was working at least two jobs to take care of her family. Walter was in the hospital with a stomach ailment and couldn't work, and Margrit needed money to pay for the babysitter and for my parents' ticket to America when it came their turn. We all needed the visa process to speed up, for the political situation did not look good.

In the middle of March, there were newsreels of sullen-faced Czechs watching German soldiers enter Prague. The occupation was quick and the repercussions deadly. Upon seeing those news reels, Herbert didn't wait for the next mail plane to deliver a letter to me. He sent me an urgent telegram.

War inevitable. Hitler will not stop. Get out of Europe immediately.
  Herbert

That telegram, and Hitler's conquest of Czechoslovakia, depressed me for days. The snow melted in Europe that spring, but our fears did not, and you needed two things to flee the continent - a visa and money. It was hard to say which was more hopelessly out of reach in 1939.

My weeks were terribly busy and sometimes it wasn't until Saturday that I had a chance to write to Herbert. I tried to remember things that I wanted to tell him, but then I would forget them by the time I was able to take out a clean piece of stationery and begin my letter. I don't think Herbert realized it, but he could sit down at his typewriter whenever he felt like it, and I couldn't.

Finally, Mrs. Bathhurst agree to give me one day off a week, and on my free days, I began to ride the train to London and try to get visas for my parents. It cost 500 pounds per person to bring a relative to England that spring, so in order to save my parents, I would need twice that, though I was making just four pounds a month.

At that rate, it would take me … twenty years.

My grandmother's brother had married the daughter of an Episcopalian minister, and their son lived in Hempstead, not far from London. He and his wife – the Freunds - were my mother's first cousins. On one of my days off, I called them, and Mrs. Freund answered.

"You are who again?" she asked coldly.

"I am Rosemarie Marienthal, Gertrude's daughter," I said in German, because it would take me a long time to say that in English and I'd probably say it wrong.

"You know, my husband's family has not lived in Germany for

quite some time," Mrs. Freund said, "and I am quite perplexed by the reason for this phone call."

When I suggested we meet for coffee, she didn't answer. Finally Mrs. Freund relented and agreed to meet me at Victoria Station a few days later. She didn't invite me to her house.

When I met her at the station, Mrs. Freund was wearing a black net around her hair, and she limply extended her hand. It was gloved. Black gloved with open fingertips.

My cousin motioned for me to sit down on the bench and did the same. Then she tapped her leg in annoyance and fingered the silver cross around her neck.

"My parents are trying to escape."

"I assure you that your parents' affair is none of ours."

"But they're desperate."

"In this country, both you and your Fuhrer are considered the enemy."

"We are not enemies. We are victims. We're Jews."

My cousin listened politely for about a moment more and then rose to her feet. "I'm sure you don't understand the demands on my time," she said. "I am very busy and not in the habit of helping relatives on the dole. I would advise you not to call upon us again."

As I rode the train back to High Wycombe and stared blankly out the window, I was struck by the irony of it all. Freund is a German word, and in English it means friend.

20 March 1939

My dearest Herbert,

I waited so long for the mail man and today there was no letter for me. Not a nice letter from you or my parents and I really need to get news from either one. At the moment I'm in real emotional trouble like never before in my life. I can't get myself to write to people who don't mean anything to me, but I do want to write to you. I am so tired of fighting, and especially at the moments where I need all my energy. The people I know here are very much involved in their own worries and don't have time to try to help me solve my problems.

You and I both know that war is coming, but if I accept your offer to work for you and do manage to acquire a visa, I would be unable to return here if the arrangement is not what we both expect. The flood of refugees to Great Britain makes reentry impossible right now, especially for those with a J on their passport. It certainly is difficult these days to be born a Jew, but you can't do anything about it.

What if you don't like me or I don't like it in Africa? My visa gives me permission for only one entry into England, and I have used that up.

Well, I must go. I have a huge basket of laundry waiting patiently for me!

Rosemarie

I pulled out the wrinkled shirts one by one from the laundry basket, sprinkled them with a bottle of water, and hurriedly raced across them with the iron. I wanted to iron each piece – dress, shirt and pants – and hang them up until the basket was empty and I could rush off to the post office and drop my latest letter to Herbert in the mail box.

Finally, I buttoned the last shirt on a hanger and smoothed it out. I folded up the ironing board, tucked away the iron, and then raced to the front door.

"And where do you think you're going young lady?" Mrs. Bathhurst said.

"Post office," I said, using my best English.

"I would think you had more important work to do here," Mrs. Bathhurst said, scowling.

"Finished," I said.

"Then you'll go tomorrow."

I clutched Herbert's letter and stood firm. "Today," I said.

Mrs. Bathhurst stood in the doorway. "You'll go when I say you're done and when I say it's okay to leave," she said.

"Pardon," I said, and slipped past her.

Mrs. Bathhurst raced after me, jiggling under her large chemise.

"You need to sew the curtains! Blacken the windows! There are air raid drills now, miss!"

I looked back, and thankfully Mrs. Bathhurst couldn't keep up. She was panting, and when I turned my back I heard her threatening to turn me over to the police as a German spy.

I ignored her. My walk to the post office that day was a joy, and I felt the wind sweep across my hair and face. Here I was in England, without a swastika in sight, and despite having to work for the dragon, I was free.

And, when I dropped Herbert's letter in the slot at the post office that afternoon, my spirits buoyed. I shared something with Herbert that no one else knew. It was an intimacy that I had never felt before. Something fresh like the buds on the trees I passed on my way back home. It was incredible that these feelings could stir for a person I had never met, but I knew it was not my imagination. There was someone real, tugging at my heart. Someone special south of the equator, and he was sensitive, intelligent and writing me the most beautiful letters. He begged me to come to Africa and work for him and enclosed a copy of a letter he had mailed to my parents:

Dr. Herbert Molser
Stanleyville, April 7, 1939
Belgian Congo, Africa

Most esteemed, gracious Frau, Dr. Marienthal:

By writing you a letter, it is to sincerely ask you to believe me that
I know how to differentiate between my feelings for Rosemarie and my
awareness of my responsibility towards her. I feel responsible both to you
and your daughter, and this feeling prompted my sending her a telegram
on March 18 to ask her to come over immediately.

And even if these were not days of inevitable war, it is my
conviction and also the generally held one here in the Congo that soon
enough this will probably be the case. There are things which you cannot
grasp in Germany in all their implications from there.

Should Rosemarie not be allowed to leave, you would probably regret
it, because it might not be possible for an unforeseeable period of time.
My house is always open to her, and my feelings for Rosemarie remain as
always. I am more afraid for what might happen to your daughter if she
extends her stay in England than for what might happen to her here.

This letter is well meant and comes from a sincere heart.

With respectful greetings, I remain always,

Yours,

Dr. Herbert Molser

My parents phoned me up that Sunday and Mother was crying. "First we had to say good-bye to you, and now we receive this letter. It's going to take us a long time to get over it."

"He wrote to you, Mutti?" I said, playing dumb.

"Yes!"

"It was hard enough to let you go to England," Father said, "but now comes this letter from that man expecting you to move even further away. And he scares me, Rosemarie. Even if he is very ambitious and diligent in his practice, as I am sure he is, he cannot take care of you."

"Vati, I'm not marrying him."

"I don't understand, Rosemarie," Mother said. "Why can't you just write to each other? Why do you have to go to Africa? If you keep corresponding, then you'll both have the opportunity to get to know each other."

"It's far better to take things slowly," Father said. "Stay in England where you're safe."

As I listened to my parents on the telephone, I felt my heart harden and my fingers stiffen. I had always been so obedient all my life, and whatever my parents asked me to do I had done. But, I was no longer a child and they needed to accept that. I was living on my own and working and I had learned to think for myself.

Still, I was tired of being a servant in England, and going to America right now was impossible. If I went to Africa I could at least work in a doctor's office and have some dignity. And, Africa … any continent … seemed safer than this one, for it was just a matter of time before Hitler advanced. The British knew he was coming and we were getting ready. There was an air raid drill scheduled that afternoon, and I was sewing black curtains for the windows.

Although I'd never met Herbert, I wanted to take a chance and work for him. I didn't know if I'd like the Congo, but anything would be better than working for the Bathhursts, and any continent in the world would be safer than this one.

Luckily, Mrs. Bathhurst cut my conversation short. "Oh, where is that girl when you need her!"

My next day off was one of those warm days that make you glad to be alive, what with the butterflies flitting across the yards and sunshine warming your nose. Greta and I decided to go for a walk in the park, and I stopped to admire some purple wildflowers.

"You know, Rosemarie, you can't blame them," Greta said, waiting as I stooped to pick a few flowers on our way to the park. I was hoping to press them between the sheets of my letter and send them to Herbert.

"They're frightened for you," Greta continued as I stood up, flowers in hand. "They don't know Herbert the way you do and they're horrified that you would actually leave them and surrender yourself to a total stranger. Plus, there's no turning back you know. Once you leave England, you're gone. You have a J in your passport and wouldn't be able to come back here or to Germany and they'd lose you forever."

"Well, that isn't going to happen," I said. "My parents will be thrilled to hear that I can't get a visa to the Congo. No African country will take me – even if I want to go! One country even had the nerve to ask me for an affidavit from Germany saying I had never been to jail, that I wasn't a criminal!"

Greta laughed. "We both know who the real criminals are, don't we?"

I nodded.

"But what if Herbert is not Mr. Wonderful the way you think he is?" Greta said, as we walked along the path, admiring the tulips and buttercups. "I mean, he sounds wonderful, but you won't really know until you meet him. And, if the relationship doesn't work, there's no way out for you. You'd be stuck in Africa forever, paying for your mistake."

"You sound like my parents," I said, frowning.

"Oh, come on, Rosemarie," Greta said. "I'm just trying to point out the other side. I'll race you to the swings!"

And race we did! It felt so good to scamper across the grass which stirred in the spring breeze. Greta beat me to the swings and then we scrambled on and pumped as fast as we could. Higher and higher we swung up in the air until we felt like we could touch the clouds with our feet.

We were just girls again, laughing the way we had back in our hometowns before we ever heard the name Adolf Hitler. As we pumped our feet into the air, racing each other higher into the sky, it felt like everything we needed was a toe-touch away. A thousand pounds, visas to England, and our families. We forgot all the horrible worries about what our future held.

10 April 1939

My dearest Herbert,

I am just back from a walk to the post office. Many, many cordial thanks for your kind letter which arrived as a belated Easter surprise. Your optimism, thank God, is contagious and I am no longer so thoroughly despairing like yesterday.

Do you think that we will find a way out despite everybody? Up to now I never wrote to you and even did not want to admit it to myself, but now that destiny threatens to forever separate us, I realize how much I care for you. It is incredible that this can happen with a person one has never met before and still I know that it is not imagination

Don't judge my parents so harshly. I wrote and told them that they will be destroying my whole life if they keep throwing obstacles into my way, after which I received a long letter from my father in which he advised me again to wait. The more I feel that my parents don't want me to go to Africa, the more I want to!

Rosemarie

Finally, in the middle of April, my parents called. I was crying for joy and could not say a word. My parents didn't mention Herbert at all. Instead they said that it was my mother's birthday and had I remembered?

Actually, I was so overworked that I hardly knew what day it was anymore, but I couldn't admit that to them. Birthdays were special in our family, and how could I forget?

My mother read me Father's latest poem to her, and the

distance and anger between us evaporated.

April 17 is here again
The joyous day and a day of lights
You are living
And even after heavy gales bend me down
You I have, and, therefore, none to fear.

We are assembled today, just two of us left –
No longer at the round table with the lamp's reddish glow,
But Margrit and Rosemarie also celebrate with us
Longing in spirit to be next to us.

We will again find our lofty ways
Even if the ground is hard as a rock – we stand firm.

"Oh Mutti, that is so beautiful!" I said, and for a moment I forgot all about the argument on the phone that previous Sunday. And, it suddenly occurred to me that to go so far away would be to abandon my parents, because there was probably no way I could help them from Africa. I would be stabbing my parents in the back, and pretending that they didn't mean anything to me when in fact they did.

Anyone could see that my parents only wanted the best for me. I didn't want to say good-bye or hang up the phone, and that night I told Herbert about their call.

20 April 1939

My most beloved Herbert,

I no longer had the feeling of being away so far and out of reach when I heard their dear voices. It is already eleven o'clock at night, but I am too happy just to sleep and I want you to participate in it.

Only now do I really feel what you are for me and what you mean for me. Simply everything, for my whole life would be empty without you.

Rosemarie

CHAPTER SEVENTEEN

Rosemarie

I T W A S G E T T I N G H A R D E R and harder to play
the role of servant because Mrs. Bathhurst ordered me around all
the time, without any consideration for my feelings. One night four
guests slept over, and it was a mess beyond one's imagination. People
camped out in the dining room and living room, and they didn't
wake up until 11 o'clock the following morning. When I tried to go
downstairs to do my morning chores, a woman screamed. How dare
I wake her?

The last straw was a nephew, who arrived at the front door
with a heavy suitcase. He was just about my age, and he set down
his bulging brown bag with relief, for the suitcase was heavy. Then,
the nephew asked me to carry it upstairs for him! I knew enough
English to understand what he was asking, and I was so taken aback
that I huffed off to the kitchen. Finally, the nephew rapped on the
kitchen door and asked when I was going to help him.

"Never," I said.

I was so alone, stuck in a miserable English household, and nobody had any idea what was going on in my life besides Herbert. Luckily I was so busy that I didn't have too much time to think about how awful my everyday life was, or to dwell on how unhappy I was.

I didn't know English well enough to help myself find a new job yet, so I started going to the movies. I would sit through the same British or American movie several times. At first, I understood just a little of what the actors and actresses said to each other, but I understood a little more the second and third time around. It wasn't the usual way people learn English. Still, it worked. I also read everything I could. I would sneak books or magazines away from my employers and try to read them at night. First I used a dictionary, looking up practically every word. Soon I would recognize words I'd already learned and spend less time flipping through the dictionary.

After six weeks of watching movies and memorizing words, I could better make myself understood. I wasn't fluent, and my German accent was thick, but I had enough English to get by at the police station, which I visited at the end of May. I wanted to find out if Mrs. Bathhurst really could send me back to Germany. I walked up the half dozen cement steps and into the brownstone building that served as the police department. There, in the front of a small office with green and white linoleum tiles, sat a constable behind a large cherry desk.

He was a happy looking fellow with reddish curls, ruddy cheeks and freckles on his arms and nose. When I asked the constable if Mrs. Bathhurst could send me back to Germany, he laughed – whether it was at the question or my halting English.

"Send you back?" he repeated, leaning back in his chair. "Why miss, you give the old lady more power than the prime minister! I know that woman, because she has quite a reputation, and that woman's a witch! How on earth did you come to work for her?"

"Through an ad, sir."

"Well, young lady, you are not the first to walk through her door, nor would you be the last one to pack up your bags. That woman cannot hold onto help anymore than Hitler can keep a promise! I'd find another job if I were you! And when you do find a new job, miss, I'll drive you there myself in my police car just to get even with the old witch!"

"Danke! Danke!" I said to the constable. "I mean, thank you!"

The constable flicked his wrist and waved me away. "Pshaw," he said. "It wasn't anything, miss!"

It was, though. I turned and ran out the door and headed downtown to the Woburn House. It was a Jewish community center in London, with a German Jewish Aid Committee for Jewish refugees. A counselor at the Jewish Aid Committee advised me to rent a flat for a week and post an ad for a new job. The advice from the aid committee, coupled with the constable's encouragement, emboldened me. I was now determined to leave my current employers and find a new job as soon as possible.

That night, I counted my savings on my bed. I had set aside six pounds from my wages. It wasn't much, but it seemed like a small fortune to me. Six pounds meant I could rent a small room for a month, and I vowed to do it so I could find another job. Greta had already found herself a better job, working for a wealthy family out in the country.

I decided to leave my job that Saturday. It was my day off and I would collect the wages that were due me and say good-bye.

That Saturday, I hurried out with my two suitcases and didn't bother to say good-bye, for I didn't care what the dragon thought when she discovered I was gone.

Out in the street, I picked up a copy of the London Times and turned to the classifieds to look up the advertisements for furnished rooms. I found one that very day and moved in. I could rent it by the month or week, and I chose to stay there a week until I found another job. It cost me a pound, and it was worth it.

The following Monday I placed an ad of my own in the paper. "Governess looking for a job with children."

Being a maid hadn't exactly worked out, but maybe being a governess would. After all, I'd had governesses all my life and knew what they were supposed to do. You just took the children to the park or zoo and kept them out of their parents' hair. Surely I could do that. I paid two pounds for the ad and waited, but I didn't have to wait long.

CHAPTER EIGHTEEN

Rosemarie

WHEN I MET LILLY HARRISON at the
interview, she didn't look much older than I was. She lived in a small
cottage in Ewell on the south side of London with a tiny green
lawn encircled by a tall white fence out back. Her home was close to
Croyden Airport, and the heart of London was close and accessible
by train.

Lilly's home was like she was - charming inside and out. The
walls were painted a cheery yellow, and flowers bloomed everywhere.
Pink and blue hydrangeas grazed happily in the sun on the walk to
the front door, and sunflowers rose by the backyard fence. Inside,
there were bouquets of daisies in blue-and-white vases. There were
antique tables and blue and white china lamps on either side of the
sofa in the living room, and the sofa was a blue toile with yellow and
blue needlepoint throw pillows.

Lilly took off her black patent leather heels and tucked her feet under her on the sofa. She was as slender and elegant as a rose, and her stomach was the only thing that bulged.

Lilly was pregnant. She tucked a strand of long sandy brown hair behind her ears and began the interview. I answered all the questions politely, but couldn't take my eyes off a photograph on her table. Lilly was stunning. She wore a glittering ball gown, and curtsied before the Queen. I could tell it was the Queen because King Edward stood at her side.

When Lilly caught me staring at the photograph, she said, "Yes, it's who you think it is. My family is a distant relative of the King's, and we have been to Buckingham Palace. My parents hoped that I'd marry into the Royal Family." She laughed nervously and looked away.

She regained her composure and told me she was looking for a governess for Rose, who had just turned 4. Rose rocked back and forth in a little white chair, sucking on her thumb and blanket and studying me. She had curly blond hair, and she wore a red cotton dress with short puffy sleeves and white smocking across the chest. There were little black poodles embroidered across the smocking of her dress, and a real poodle rested at her feet.

Rose didn't know it, but I had brought her a present. I had bought it without ever having met her, just so I could make a good impression. I reached down at my feet and pulled out a little fur monkey from my shopping bag. It was a puppet.

I squatted next to Rose and touched the monkey's nose gently to hers and was rewarded with two rows of tiny white teeth. Rose tucked her chin in and looked up at me with her blue eyes. The poodle sniffed at me and wagged its tail.

"Are you Jewish?" Lilly asked.

The question caught me off guard. It was a bold question, and

I blinked, but when I turned my head and looked into Lilly's eyes, I beheld only tenderness and compassion.

I nodded.

"Well, then you aren't a friend of Hitler's any more than we are!" Lilly said. "And, you will get along well with our maid!"

The cleaning woman, it turned out, was another Jewish refugee from Vienna. Oh how many of us there were, frantically seeking refuge.

Lilly didn't need me to do housework as I'd done at the Bathhursts. Instead, she was looking for someone to be a companion and governess to her daughter because soon she would be very busy.

Lilly patted her stomach and smiled warmly. "I am going to need help, and I'd love it to be you."

Lilly was so slender and her stomach so tiny that I didn't realize how advanced she was in her pregnancy. The baby was due the beginning of July and it arrived on July 8. It was a boy, and he was born at home with the help of the midwife. Lilly's husband celebrated by getting drunk that night and staggering home, singing. He often smelled of whiskey and slept off a night's drinking, missing work.

Even though she was exhausted from the birth, Lilly still thought of me. "Why don't you call your parents and tell them our good news, and let me pay for the call!" she said.

My mother answered the phone in Bochum, and my skin tingled with joy to hear her voice once more.

"We're trying very hard to get our papers to go to America, but it isn't progressing very well," Mother said. "Thank goodness we're not on that ship the St. Louis, though. Then we would really be in trouble."

"The St. Louis?"

"The ship we wanted Margrit to take. The one that sailed to Cuba last May."

"What happened, Mutti? Sometimes I'm so busy I don't hear all the news."

"Well, there were nine hundred Jews from Europe on board, and Cuba wouldn't let most of them off the ship. The passengers were hoping to stay in Cuba until their visas to America cleared. At least there they'd be safe and close to the United States. But the Cuban government wouldn't let the ship dock, and the captain cruised along the coast of Florida, hoping America would give the okay. President Roosevelt refused, and the St. Louis had to sail back to Europe."

"Mutti, that's so sad!"

"Oh, that's not the worst of it either. Some of the passengers felt so hopeless that they jumped. They preferred drowning to returning to Hamburg."

I felt sorry for them and for all of us. "It seems we're all in the same boat, whether we're on land or sea," I told Mother. "We're Jews and the war is so close, and I don't know how this will end."

"It doesn't look like much hope of peace around here, does it?" Mother said.

"I can't believe that this terrible war is coming. If only it was all a bad dream and we could wake up and be together again. What will happen to us if war comes? How will I reach you?"

Mother had no answers, nor did my father either. "We've just got to hope that we all make it to America soon," Vati said.

19 July 1939

My dearest Herbert,

I'm quite happy here. Mrs. Harrison is very nice and I don't have too much to do. Mostly the little one follows me wherever I go! It's good that

I have learned to speak English because a child that's 4 years old asks a lot of questions!

Of course I'm terribly worried about the political situation. I'm not sure what Hitler intends to do and everyone is very pessimistic. The whole world is upset with what Hitler is doing and I don't understand it all together. I really don't see how this can end well. I think Europe wants to buy peace and I think that Hitler has something altogether different in mind and that this is going to end up in a blood bath.

There is so much we have to talk about once we meet up with each other and I hope that it could be soon. I really want it so much. I believe and I hope that everything will work out all right and that eventually we'll have a good life together and share many things we both love.

Good night and dream of me. I was already in bed and then I remembered that I want to send you a good night kiss.

Rosemarie

12 August, 1939

My darling girl,

My mother always said that things have a way of turning out for the best, and only now do I understand that. I was engaged to a Swiss woman before I met you, and we broke it off because she was not Jewish and the Nazis forbade our relationship. I'm now glad we broke it off because I see that if I had married that young woman, I would have never met the delightful girl with whom I have shared all my thoughts and feelings this past year.

Work on that visa, Rosemarie. I really love it here and can't wait for you to see it. I know you will come to the same end result that I did, that this is a beautiful spot to live.

When you do come here, I want you to do two things. When you see that I don't have many patients, which unfortunately is the case, please

108

don't ask me why. It makes me so sad that I can't talk about it. Some patients won't come to me because I'm German, which grieves me so. In the last eight months, there were many days when I had no patients at all and it saddened me. It especially grieves me because I feel very responsible for you if you decide to come.

I do hope you will come, not just to end my loneliness, but for your sake as well. You have brought such joy to my life, and I would like to return that favor and bring all that joy to you.

Herbert

That August, I told Lilly everything about Herbert, for it was impossible for her not to notice that I had a boyfriend. To whom was I writing, and who was sending me all these letters from Africa? I had no relatives there, and yet a new letter would show up on our doorstep every day with the same postmark. Stanleyville.

Lilly smiled as she handed me the latest letter. "Well, well, here's another one from abroad! You seem to have charmed someone down south of the equator, and he must be quite smitten! Surely all these letters aren't from a brother."

"No. I don't have any brothers."

"A cousin, perhaps?"*

"No, not a cousin. "

"A boyfriend, then?"

"Well, not exactly," I said, eyelashes downcast with embarrassment. Gert had been the only boyfriend I'd ever had. I still thought about him, and I'd written to his parents and asked for his address. Mrs. Freudenberg wrote me right back and gave it to me, and she told me to be on the lookout for Gert at the Woburn House, because he spent all his free time there trying to help them. At night, I'd sometimes try to picture Gert, remembering his face, his eyes, and his smile. Gert was still clear to me, and I could envision him. Herbert was just a dream.

"You see," I said, looking up at Lilly and continuing. "I haven't actually met this man yet. We just write to each other."

"A pen pal, then," Lilly said.

"Well, he's more than that."

"Oh. Yes. Of course! Quite right!" Lilly said, and smiled.

15 August, 1939

My dearest Herbert,

The political situation is terrible. One doesn't know what's going to happen. On my days off, I go to the various government embassies to check on my visa. I am never the only wretch there, either. There are throngs of refugees, all day long. The whole of European humanity is scurrying around trying to find shelter before the war.

I'm still thinking that maybe I can go with the German shipping lines to Africa. I talked to one man at the shipping office, and I asked him what would happen to the German boats on their way to Africa if there is a war. The shipping official said that they would probably have to be interned in a port. That would be better than to be sent back to Hamburg like those poor souls on the St. Louis, though. We are all very lucky that my brother-in-law didn't pay for that trip to Cuba. If he had, my sister and brother-in-law and their baby would have all been sent back to Hamburg and ended up in the camps.

If only we could speed up my visa! If I don't leave soon, and the war starts, then it's over for the two of us forever and we will both have to see how we can manage our lives without each other. It would be simply too sad and terrible if everything we have built this past year, with thousands of dear thoughts, were now to crumble like a fragile boat against this insuperable cliff.

Rosemarie

P.S. – Lilly took a photograph of me the other week, and I wanted to share it with you. Please send me one of you as well!

20 August 1939

My beloved girl,

Your picture is in front of me on the table. You asked me if I ever encountered a woman like you, and I can tell you with my whole heart never. But, now that I have, without thinking about it I would ask her to marry me. I have never said yes to any person in my life like I am saying it to you. I am gaining new patients from India, who don't hold a grudge against me because I'm German, the way the Belgians do. My medical practice is starting to grow and I will be even happier if I can share my life with you. I can only imagine that if we live together it would be wonderful!

I do not know what will happen with this war, but pray that it will draw you to me!

Herbert

26 August, 1939

My dearest Herbert,

Thank you for the photograph you sent me. Your dear picture is now my best friend, and I tell you everything at night. When I'm especially weary after a long exhausting day, I cry in front of your picture. But, most of the time I don't have time to cry! Our new born baby doesn't allow anyone to sleep in this house. I really don't have any peace day or night because the lady from Vienna who works here with me is sick so I'm stuck with all her work. I'm back to being a domestic, and can barely keep my eyes open.

Times like these make me long to take you up on your offer to come to Africa. Still, if I were to come to Africa, I would need to sail from Antwerp. That entails a visa, and my visa to Brussels was refused without any explanation. I'm going to send my application to my aunt in Brussels and ask her if she can do something for me. I have a feeling that it's too late now because I heard that if there is a war, all sailing trips will be cancelled. If there is a war and I can't get out anymore, will you let me know how you are? I care about you and always want to know that you're well.

All my love,

Rosemarie

I WAS WASHING the baby's diapers and hanging them outside to dry when the Prime Minister announced on the radio that he had lost all hope of getting Hitler to back down from war with Poland. I immediately telephoned my parents and we were overjoyed to hear each other's voices.

"The war is close, Mutti, and you have got to leave now before it's too late!"

"I know, Rosemarie, and Vati and I are both now ready to get out of Germany," said Mother, sounding a bit tired. "Our number is getting close in Stuttgart. They have called 224,000 and we are not far behind."

"If only it will be called soon," I said anxiously. "In England the atmosphere is very dangerous and feels like war. I'm very afraid. We have got to see each other again!"

"When we are able to leave, Vati and I will build a new life in

America and hopefully you will join us. For now, I am happy that I at least have your father, and that Heidi is still with us. Otherwise we would be all alone."

"How is Heidi doing?"

"She is getting tired of Mrs. Kaminsky living here! Still, Heidi has the courage of a young person and we need that. I have begun packing up some things, and when Vati sees me he says that he hopes a move will be temporary and that we can come back someday."

"But Mutti, will Germany ever be the place we knew when we were younger?"

"When Hitler is forced out of office, I think it can be," Mutti said. "Father and I talk a lot about the past, about how wonderful it was."

Two days later I walked into a small store with Rose, on the premise that I wanted to buy her a lollipop, but it was really to read the latest news. Inside the store that Friday, the smell of must and tobacco brushed past me and I gripped Rose's hand.

"Let's see if we can find you a treat," I told her.

There were stacks of newspapers lining the checkered floor, and the shop owner didn't notice me scanning the newspaper headlines. He stood at attention, listening to a small black radio plugged in on the counter. His head bowed and his chin drooped. He stared vacantly at his hairy, folded hands.

"Attention. Attention. German forces have invaded Poland and its planes have bombed Polish cities, including the capital, Warsaw. The attack comes without any warning or declaration of war."

I gasped and tried to shield my terror from Rose.

"Britain and France have mobilized their forces and are preparing to wage war on Germany for the second time this century." I did not disturb the shopkeeper. I helped Rose pick out a red lollipop and

then chose the Times of London for myself. I laid the proper shillings on the counter and quietly slipped out. Londoners gathered in store fronts, straining to hear the news.

The worst of all possible fears had come true. I felt terrible for my parents at home, and I couldn't believe the German people didn't open their eyes to see what was being done to them. I ran straight home.

"Lilly, the Nazis ... invaded ... Poland" I whispered, my heart pounding after my homeward sprint. Lilly patted the baby's back to burp him and walked quietly around the living room.

She pointed to the gas masks lying on the coffee table. The government mined the English Channel to stop a German attack by sea, and passed out gas masks to protect everyone in case of an attack by air.

"So, old Neville was right," Lilly said. "I guess we'll be wearing these frightful things after all."

We gathered up our gas masks, and practiced trying them on. With their plastic eye sockets and long black snouts, the rubber gas masks we received made Lilly, Rose and I look like creatures from outer space. There was even a glass box in which to place the baby to protect him from a toxic gas attack. It looked like a glass cabinet, and it was as terrifying to us as it was to the baby when we placed him inside. We had to pump in fresh air as if we were in the middle of a German attack.

We were also asked not to turn on any lights at night unless it was absolutely necessary. And we were required to hang our black-out curtains in front of every window. The reason was that city lights would make us sitting ducks for Nazi bombs.

War was coming, and Lilly kept the radio on all afternoon. Two days later, Chamberlain declared that England would stand up and defend Poland. Hitler had better withdraw his troops or prepare for war.

Meantime, Lilly and I followed government orders and prepared the basement for an air raid shelter. If German planes attacked London, the country wanted to be prepared. England wasn't so much afraid of invasion by land as it was by air. After all, the channel was like a moat.

The British Broadcasting Company informed everyone of the upcoming air alert drill that very Sunday afternoon. I piled up blankets and pillows and hauled them down to the basement for the drill. I was terribly afraid that the whole continent would end up in a blood bath.

1 September, 1939

My dearest Herbert,

Today the most horrible thing has happened. It's awful, but war had to come. We saw it coming, and we didn't doubt that Hitler could do it. I went up to my room and cried.

War will be a catastrophe, and I can't imagine how life can go on – especially for my parents. Now it looks like it will be years before we will be able to see each other as well. With all our strength we must try to fight to see each other. I never saw you but still I'm sure that we could be good friends. I don't know if I love you, but I have the feeling that I could. Why does fate deny people the chance to get together?

The girl from Vienna who is with me told me that even the worst winter eventually ends, and that not every bullet hits somebody, and we have to hope that nothing will hit us. Sometimes it takes much more courage to continue on living than to take your own life.

This will be a short letter because I'm going to try to write to my parents through the neutral countries. Our chances to see each other are definitely greater than the chance that we will see our parents again. In case you haven't thought of it, perhaps you could write to your parents and

send the letter to Mr. Guttentag or my aunt, and they can forward it on
to Germany.

I'm going to continue to try to get out of here, but in case something
should happen to me, I will give your address to Mrs. Harrison so that
you can hear.

Day and night my thoughts are with you, and eventually everything
will work out all right. Don't lose courage that there is going to be a better
tomorrow.

Rosemarie

When I fell asleep that night, I dreamed that I was back in our
kitchen in Bochum when suddenly the garden door swung open and
Herbert walked in. It was the first time I had ever seen him, and he
was tall with dark hair and a dimpled-chin. The dimple was a sign
of the vulnerability within. Herbert was all alone, and he needed
me just as much as I needed him. I reached up to kiss him and he
grabbed me and pulled me close. We kissed awkwardly at first, but
then our lips locked and our feelings of clumsiness were swept away.

"Don't stop," Herbert said, and I didn't want to either. I was
flooded with the warmth of that kiss and a feeling of happiness
greater than I had ever known, and a feeling of safety as well.

CHAPTER TWENTY

BRITAIN DECLARED WAR on Germany, and telephone and mail service ended to home. My parents could no longer call me as they had each Sunday, and Lilly handed me my last letter to them. The post man had returned it with the mail. My letter was stamped "undeliverable," and its flap was still sealed.

As I sat in a big chair in Lilly's living room, reading the letter I had written to my parents, my eyes were downcast and my heart felt like it had sunk into the carpet.

"These are the toughest of times, aren't they?" Lilly asked gently, watching me.

I looked up at the ceiling, and tried my best to dam the tears. "I feel cut off now," I said. "I'm here with you but I can no longer help my parents. I might as well be in America or Africa. It makes no difference anymore because there is nothing I can do for them."

The German refugees who arrived right before the borders closed said that food was being rationed and Jews were receiving the least. Their rations were small and they were starving.

"Lilly, could I have the afternoon off?" I asked, eyes clouding as I stared off at a picture above the fireplace. I had to see what I could do for my parents.

Of course Lilly agreed, and I offered to take Rose with me to give Lilly some rest with the baby. Lilly laid down for a nap, and I wheeled Rose down to the British immigration office in her navy pram. I wondered if I'd see Gert, because I knew he had to be just as worried about his parents, and I took my place at the end of a very long line that wrapped around the brick building.

The man ahead of me closed his eyes and then pulled his hat down low over his forehead. His chin tucked down toward his chest and his arms were crossed. The man hugged himself and rocked back and forth, and the fringes of a prayer shawl hung down beneath his torn jacket. He appeared to be praying.

When the man ahead of me stopped, his eyes opened and they were red around the rims. The wind blew past us and carried his hat with it. I ran forward to get it and handed it back to the man. It was then that I saw his yarmulke.

"Thank you," he said, mouthing the words in English.

"You're welcome," I said in my best English. "It's a rather long line, isn't it?"

The man responded in English but his words had a distinctly heavy Polish accent. "Yes,' he said quietly. "My sister lives in Tarnopol, and I haven't heard a word. Its been about a week now and I'm a little worried. We usually talk once a week, but we knew the war was coming and she promised to call and let me know how she was doing when it broke out. I tried to call her, but the operator said there was no longer any phone service to Poland. All lines were cut and I haven't heard a word. It's a little scary because her home is where the Nazis started bombing. I didn't know what to do, and I was going crazy. Finally I said I'll just risk it and go back home and make sure she's okay, if the British will let me."

The couple ahead of the Polish man were Americans, gathering an exit visa for New York. The couple behind me were Belgian, eager to return to Antwerp. With war threatening to engulf all of us, the eyes around me were sad and frightened.

How long was the line now? I excused myself to check and hurried around the corner. The throng of people extended all the way along the side of the building to the staircase leading up to the immigration office.

I studied all the faces, wondering where they came from and where they were headed and what their stories were. I looked from cheek to cheek, from each sunken pair of eyes to the next, when all of a sudden I saw a familiar pair of eyes, the dark lock of hair that dipped over the eyebrows, and the navy blazer now several inches too short and worn.

I gasped.

"Gert!" I screamed, running as fast as I could to catch him. He didn't hear me at first but then he turned his head just as I reached him and threw my arms around him.

Slowly Gert wrapped his arms around me, and I could feel him breathing on the top of my hair. He kissed the top of my head and tried to squeeze me tight, but his arms felt awkward. I pulled back to kiss his cheek and it felt cold.

"Rosemarie," he said looking at me with both joy and sadness. "I wondered if we'd run into each other here. My mother wrote that you had taken a job in London and that you often came here."

"You didn't try to get my phone number? To call me?" I asked, puzzled. "I wrote your parents a number of times to ask how you were."

Gert's eyes fell down to a crack in the sidewalk. "I…" He shuffled the toe of his shoes on a crack and then looking up at me. "Rosemarie, I haven't been myself since Sachsenhausen, and all I can think of is getting my parents out of Germany. I'm sorry."

"Your mother said that you were staying with a Jewish family in Sussex. How do you like them?" I asked.

"They're … okay," Gert said. "I think they would have preferred a younger child. The younger ones got snapped up, though, and I was one of the last ones left."

"Left?"

"Not selected right away. It's kind of like being in an orphanage and sitting politely on the benches, hoping a family will like you."

"So, how is it going?" I asked.

"It's … okay," Gert said. "I try to leave as early as possible and work as much as possible to avoid overstaying my welcome. I feel guilty living off them, not being a child, you know. I don't want to take advantage of anyone, but I need the place to stay, so I can work and save up money for my parents."

"You're working?"

He said he was cleaning dishes in the back of a small restaurant not far from his host family. I winced as I looked up at Gert, listening to him talk. For there was only a trace of the Gert I remembered. Gert had lost weight, even more than he had even lost in Sachsenhausen, and his eyes were sorrowful.

We stood in line together for a few moments, chatting, and Gert shifted from one foot to the other. His pants were a couple of inches short and frayed at the hem. Gert looked as if he was the last recipient of a pair of hand-me-downs that would not survive this final wear. He strained his neck above the crowd to gauge how much further we had to wait for the front of the line, and twisted his papers in his hand. Soon I ran out of questions and Gert stopped talking. He stared down at the toes of his shoes.

"Gert, are you all right?"

"All right? Rosemarie, how can I possibly be all right when my parents are back in Germany with no way out!"

"I know, Gert. My parents are still there, too."

"I've been working as many hours as I can, trying to save up the thousand pounds the Nazis want to let them go, but all I have are seventy-two pounds to show for eight months work. And, I've spent nothing. Nothing!"

"Gert, you're doing the best you can. We all are."

"But you don't understand, Rosemarie. I've got to get my parents out! And now, with the war, I may be too late!"

Gert was right, for the British government would never allow German Jews in to the country now. They were canceling all visas to enemy nationals, and that meant us, even if we were Jewish refugees.

"Mein Gott, what will I do?" Gert said, his eyes misting at the corners. "What will become of my parents?"

I reached up to hug him again, but his arms were stiff. Still, I could only imagine how hard it must be for him to be an only child. My sister Margrit was doing everything she could to get our parents out of Germany, and it was a comfort to know there were two of us to tow the load. As for Gert, all the responsibility fell on him, for there was no one else, and, I could find no words to console him that day.

"Well, I'd better go back in line," I said. "Good luck, Gert."

"You know, Rosemarie, you'd better be careful," Gert said, looking down at me with those wounded eyes. "You've got a J in your passport and that's dangerous."

"I don't think so," I said. "Not here."

Gert's hand touched my coat sleeve and he looked me straight in the eye. "Listen, Rosemarie. You and I are Jews, and what's worse, we're German Jews. Now that there's a war on, we need a special permit to stay here. And, the British aren't going to wait for the Nazis to round us up because they'll do it first. The British are going to send 40,000 immigrants back to Germany, and the ones they can't send back, they're going to put in jail, just like they're doing to the immigrants trying to get into Palestine. The British don't like Jews any more than Hitler does, but they're a little more discreet about it."

I took a few steps backward. "No," I said. "That's not true."

"Palestine," Gert said, nodding his head with a knowing look in his eyes. "Ask someone about Palestine, and be careful."

I nodded as well and kept on walking, and then I turned and did not look back.

Upon my return home to Lilly, I told her what Gert had said. "What's worse is that my German citizenship makes me the enemy now."

"That's ridiculous," Lilly said, nuzzling the head of the baby as she held him close to her chest.

"Ridiculous or not," I said, "war changes everything. The Germans may brand me with a J on my passport, but I'm an enemy alien all the same. And now I have to apply for a special identity card."

"It's awful," Lilly said. "If only Chamberlain can get Hitler to back down and maintain peace."

On my next day off, I let Lilly rest, and I wheeled Rose and the baby down to the local police station to take care of my identity card. I didn't mind registering with the police, for the constable was my friend! He greeted me with a warm "Hullo!", listened with a smile to my tale of deserting the Bathhursts, and congratulated me on my new family.

"Served them right!" the constable said, handing a lollipop to Rose. "I'm glad you walked out on your employers. Bloody lot of snoots they were!"

Luckily, England was not at war with the Belgian Congo, and mail service to Africa was not disturbed. I wrote Herbert that very night.

> 5 September 1939
>
> *My dearest Herbert,*
>
> *I am ready to leave Europe and be with you, but I'm afraid that I'm stuck here in England for this war has spoiled everything. My parents warned me to go to America as soon as I could if war broke out. They even managed to buy me a ticket to New York by ship, and they urged me to join Margrit as soon as I could round up my visa. They told me they'd follow as soon as they could, but I don't want to stay in England any longer than I have to. I'm scared.*
>
> *I get no mail from Germany anymore and I'm terribly worried about my parents. People who just came from Germany to England said that Germany is not treating the Jews any worse right now and that so far they are being allowed into bomb shelters whenever there is fear of an Allied attack.*
>
> *I just got a card from my aunt in Brussels. The good news is that the Belgian consulate will grant me a visa, and it's amazing that my aunt was able to accomplish this. It is really a miracle that in the middle of a war I can get a visa. God must be helping us.*
>
> *My new employer is very nice to me and is helping me, too. She is a very lovely and very smart woman who acts more like a friend than a supervisor. She completely understands the situation for me with the way*

things are going in Europe, and she can see why I want to get away from here as soon as I can.

It is a difficult decision for me, Herbert, but I think I'm ready to come to Africa now. Try to wish me that everything works out, although it will be months before I can save up enough money for a boat ticket.

Rosemarie

Herbert didn't waste time responding. In his next letter, he not only sent me a boat ticket, but also an airplane ticket from Brussels to the African city of Matadi! Herbert also enclosed a ticket on a river boat from Leopoldville to Stanleyville, the town where he lived.

"An airplane ticket! Who flies in an airplane besides Charles Lindbergh! You're a lucky, lucky girl Rosemarie," Lilly said.

Lilly studied my ticket quietly, trying to read every word and savor it. Lilly had been raised in a privileged home, but even she had never seen an airplane ticket before. "I should rejoice for you, but I'm also a little sad. I'm going to miss you," she said. Slowly Lilly extended her arm and handed me back my ticket. Her eyes were glazed.

12 September 1939

Dear Herbert,

Thank you so much for the tickets, but I feel terrible that you spent all your hard earned money on me! Promise me that when we meet each other, if you're disappointed or I'm disappointed, we're going to call the whole thing quits. If you have doubts or I have doubts after that first encounter, we have to tell each other honestly, even if it will hurt. Better a quick finish than a horrible thing without ending. We have to give ourselves an out if we need it.

Don't think badly about me that I write this to you, and I must

run because the mailbox will be emptied momentarily. A thousand dear
regards and hold me dearly.

    Rosemarie

15 September 1939
Dearest Rosemarie,

    The money is inconsequential for I only hope that you will soon be
on your way. I can't tell you how happy I will be when you escape. All
I can tell you is that I would have waited for you for years or as long as
necessary because you are my heart. I only hope that our struggle will
prove that our love for each other was right. We have acted together
almost like man and wife. Our combined energy is bringing us together
and will keep us together forever. We will miss our families, but let's not
be sad – even though we will miss them desperately.

    Herbert

According to Herbert, it was benevolent destiny that we had
begun corresponding with each other. He believed that we were
destined to breathe joy and happiness into each other's lives, and
that coming together in Africa was our best means of survival
during this war. He said he couldn't wait to meet me at last and hold
me close.

Herbert said I would need an exit visa from England before I
could sail to Brussels, and he suggested that I try again for a return
permit to England just in case I needed it. To that end, I stopped by
the British immigration office in London on my next day off.

The line spilled out onto the steps and hugged the building
clear down the block. I took my place at the end of the line, and
finally, after a few hours of waiting, it was my turn to step up to the

counter. The clerk in front of me looked exhausted. Lines creased his forehead.

I began my tale in my best broken English, weighted down by my thick German accent. "Sir, I need exit visa to Africa. Also, I need return permit to England. Thank you very much."

The clerk's gray-tufted eyebrows arched and his jaw stiffened. He opened my visa, studied it for a second, and then pushed it back to me across the counter.

"Fraulein, you hold a German passport," the officer said, "and a re-entry permit is out of the question. You may leave England, if you wish, but the British government isn't exactly going to welcome you back. You are now considered an enemy alien."

"But sir," I pleaded, pointing to the J on my passport. "I am Jewish! I am not a Nazi! I am not an enemy! I need a return permit!"

The head shook, and a finger motioned me to the side. "There's a bloody war on, miss. We can't take any chances. Next!"

I lowered my eyes and threaded my way out through the flood of refugees pressing toward the counter and home.

It wasn't going to be easy getting out of Europe. My exit visa was just one of many papers I would need, as I would also need a one-week transit visa to Belgium so that I could sail there for the flight to Africa.

Thank goodness Lilly was as kind and generous as she was, because I needed several mornings off to pick up my transit papers, especially from the Belgian consulate.

"I need a transit visa," I told the consulate clerk in the best English I could muster.

The clerk, who had a pen roosted on his ear, picked up my visa and examined it. A second or two later he scowled and threw it angrily across the counter.

"Mademoiselle, it is impossible. Absolutely out of the question. We cannot issue any more transit visas to Jews. Our country is full of them. They are staying put because no one else wants them. No, a transit visa is out of the question."

His nose rose an inch or two and he looked on to the gentleman behind me, inviting him forward.

I remained where I was. "But monsieur, I am not going to stay in Belgium! I only want to stop there on my way to Africa. I need a transit visa, not a visa."

"Mademoiselle, you must step aside," said the exasperated clerk. " Look at the line behind you! And what you ask is absolutely against orders."

A throng of people stood in half a dozen lines with visas in hand, and their eyes looked just as sober and desperate as mine. There were so many souls, all with their own plight.

With a heavy heart I stepped aside and headed home. But, I knew that I would not be able to leave England and use my airplane ticket unless I had a transit visa to Belgium.

Outside, I leaned my back against the wall of the building and thought. I couldn't leave without the transit visa, so I just had to stay until closing time when the crowds died down and I had more time to make my case.

At the end of the day, though, the lines were still several people deep. "Mademoiselle, you must leave. We are closing," the clerk said.

"But sir... "

"You will have to try again in the morning."

The housekeeper from Vienna was feeling better, and she owed me some relief from my responsibilities since I had taken over for her that one time.

So the following day, I returned to the consulate an hour before it opened. When the doors were unlocked, I was welcomed in.

I repeated my story. "You don't give up, do you?" the clerk said.

"No, sir. My father told me never to give up."

"Well, your father is a smart man. So tell me. What was your situation? You have a J on your passport and wish to secure a transit visa?

"Yes, sir."

"And you are telling me the truth? That you are just passing through Belgium?"

"Yes, sir, on my way to Africa. I'm going to Africa."

"I see. Well, that is not the usual destination around here, but it is none of my business where people decide to go. And you understand how a transit visa works? That you cannot stay in the country longer than eight days?"

"Oh yes, sir! I do understand. And here is my plane ticket to Africa!"

"A plane ticket. Also quite unusual. Well I guess you wouldn't have a plane ticket unless you intended to fly now, would you?"

"No sir!"

"Very well. Because you are such a persistent, determined and courageous young lady, and because you are the lucky holder of that airplane ticket, I will issue you an eight-day transit visa. But you had better abide by the stipulations and leave the country before eight days up or you'll be deported back to Germany. Is that understood?"

"Yes, sir!"

Bang. Stamp.

I was handed my visa with a wink and a kind look. "Good luck, mademoiselle. Take good care of yourself in Africa."

CHAPTER TWENTY-ONE

Ferdinand

BY THE THIRD WEEK in September, I had gathered all the papers I needed for my journey to Africa. Now it was time to cross the English Channel and make my way to Belgium – the first leg of my journey to Herbert.

Lilly and Rose accompanied me on the train to the port of Dover. Lilly had been very good to me, and I felt guilty about abandoning her. On the pier, I swooped Rose up into my arms and squeezed her tight. Then I set her down gently and touched the tip of her nose to see her smile one more time. When I hugged Lilly, I felt a tear spill down my cheek. "Lilly, thank you for everything,"

"Oh, Rosemarie, it's been fun!" Lilly said. "I've enjoyed our time together, and I couldn't have taken care of the baby without you. By the way, I'm very jealous of you."

"Jealous?"

"Yes. Quite! You get to fly off to see this romantic doctor of yours! I'd trade places any day to escape this war!"

Lilly gave me one last squeeze. "Take care of yourself, dear girl! God be with you!"

I boarded the ferry and set my suitcases down along the rusted railing. A steward handed me an orange life preserver spotted with mildew. Soiled or not, I tied it on as quickly as I could. I wanted to remember this sight of Dover and savor it forever. I looked up at the white sandy cliffs, and across at Lilly and Rose blowing kisses my way.

I was embarking on a new adventure, but trying to hug my island sanctuary and second family one last time. I had been with my new family for so short a time, but I would not forget them.

I knew little about England when I fled Germany, and since then the British isle had become a haven to me. Now I was letting go, gambling that I would become fond of Africa as well.

On the ship's loudspeaker, the captain described the danger we'd face in the channel. Just three days ago, the British navy laid mines to blow up any invading German submarines. I snapped the top buckle on my life jacket and listened.

"'Tis a dangerous time," the captain said, as a steward reeled in the rope and anchor and the boat pulled away. "We could be blown to bits by the mines you know. The navy confided to us where they placed the mines, and we'll skirt around them as best as we bloody can. But it's still treacherous out here. Hold tight to your belongings. Wear them around your neck. Stuff them in your pockets, and God be with us."

I couldn't move. Then, I took a deep breath, removed my passport from my purse, and shoved it in my bra. My eyes darted between the captain and Lilly, and my mind between sadness and fear. I kept my eyes fixed on Lilly and Rose until they shrank to tiny specks on the pier as the ferry tooted and chugged out of the harbor. The channel churned, heaving us high and low and spraying us with icy salt water. A sharp wind whipped my cheeks red and chilled me through my jacket.

The captain warned us that there was no guarantee that we'd cross the channel safely, and he forbade us to go below deck in case we struck a mine. I was squished between passengers, and our bodies pressed against one another as the channel rudely tossed us about. There was such a hush that you could hear each other's teeth chatter. We were too scared to speak.

"Almighty God, we pray for our safe passage," a man said as we slipped through the ocean minefield. Hours later, I gasped at the beauty of the fiery orange sun, squatting comfortably on the sea like a mother hen. Then, pink and purple wisps in the sky pitched over to black, and soon, out of the shroud of darkness, glittering lights twinkled hello. Antwerp lay ahead.

Behind me a passenger whistled. Then, a man clapped, and soon we all clapped hands and cheered. The sparkling lights of Antwerp were a breathtaking sight after having lived in London during a black-out. The passengers on both sides of me slipped their hands into mine, and we held hands as the ferry quietly docked. Strangers a few hours ago, we kissed each other and embraced. We were all very thankful that we had crossed the strait safely.

"Rosemarie…"

My Tante (aunt) Marie called out my name as I walked down

the plank. Tante Marie was the widow of my Uncle Ferdinand, my father's brother. She was a short, plump woman who wore her hair in a tight gray bun. She looked like a once elegant tea cup that you couldn't bear to part with, despite its cracks and chips.

"Mon cher enfant (dear child)," Tante Marie said, embracing me. "I am so happy that you arrived safely."

"Thank you for coming to meet me, Tante Marie."

"My child, it is a pleasure. I was so excited to hear that you were coming. But, I know what a rough trip you must have had. Come. You're probably very tired. There's a 9 p.m. train to Brussels. We can catch it if we run!"

It wasn't hard keeping up with Tante Marie as we walked to the station. She paused every couple of minutes and leaned against another building. "I really must lose some weight!" she said. Then, she took a deep breath, grabbed my hand, and guided me to the train. We slid through the doors just in time and settled into the last empty seats.

Tante Marie's enormous bosom bobbed with every pant until her heart settled back to a resting beat. "I talked to your parents this morning, Rosemarie, and they're frantic. They're beside themselves, worried to death about you. You must call them as soon as we get to my apartment. I promised them that we'd call before you went to sleep."

I had forgotten that, unlike England and Germany, Belgium and Germany were not at war and there was still telephone service available between these two countries. My parents had obviously taken advantage of that, and they would not give up until they talked me out of going to Africa.

"Don't go," my aunt pleaded as the train swayed along the track. "Don't do this to yourself. You're too young. You can marry anyone you want one day, so why rush to meet a strange man so far away?

Why, you hardly know him and how can you trust him? What if he turns out to be nothing like what you expect? He could … he could… turn out to be like your Uncle Ferd."

Tante Marie turned away. A tear beaded in her eye and I knew why. My aunt had been about my same age when she met Uncle Ferdinand, one of my father's six brothers. Ferdinand was the most handsome of them all. He was extremely intelligent and high spirited, and women fawned for his attention, including Tante Marie. But, her love grew out of compassion and sympathy for a wounded man.

You see, Tante Marie met Uncle Ferdinand in a hospital in Brussels at the end of the Great War. Uncle Ferdinand had been shot in the head, and the injury to his brain nearly killed him. Though he recovered, the scar tissue to his brain caused epileptic fits for the rest of his life. Tante Marie was the chief nurse who cared for Uncle Ferdinand, and Uncle Ferdinand was touched by Tante Marie's tender care.

Soon after Uncle Ferdinand left the hospital, the two began dating, and within a year they married. Yet, despite the couple's devotion to each other, it was a difficult marriage and their relationship was doomed from the start. My Uncle Ferdinand was far more intelligent than my aunt, and he grew restless when he couldn't discuss books, world events, or philosophy with someone who could share her own insights and perceptions.

Tante Marie had come from a lower-class family, and she was out of place among my wealthy, world-traveling relatives. And, she was Christian – an unacceptable match for some of the more religious Marienthals.

But, most of all, Uncle Ferdinand was not the same man he was before the war. His quick wit was replaced by an overwhelming sadness over the frequent convulsions that wracked his body. He couldn't work and didn't feel comfortable around people. He was embarrassed to go out in public for fear of one of his attacks.

Uncle Ferdinand became a hermit. And, eight years after they had married, he shot himself. "I thought I could save his soul and make him feel better after the war," Tante Marie said. "He was handsome and kind, and I wanted desperately to cure him of his fits and depression, but I failed. He was in too much emotional pain. No one could save him, and I lost him. How many happy years did I have with him? Now I'm old and all alone."

My aunt reached over and turned my chin toward hers. "Look at me, sweetheart. I don't want you to suffer the way I have. Take a good look at me and then at this man you think you love. Don't follow your heart until it breaks, chasing after a man you hardly know."

I turned away. Although I felt bad for Tante Marie, I didn't see how Uncle Ferdinand was like Herbert. Herbert hadn't been injured during a war. He wasn't suffering from convulsions and we were surely more compatible. I was certain that I was his intellectual equal, although he was far more mature and worldly.

"But Tante Marie, don't you see how different my situation is?" I said. "I know Herbert better. We've been writing to each other for almost a year. Besides, Uncle Phillip knows Herbert very well. He wouldn't have introduced us if he wasn't certain that Herbert was a good man. Go with me tomorrow to see Uncle Phillip. Maybe then you'll see that Herbert is not at all like Uncle Ferdinand."

As soon as I said those last half dozen words, I wanted to take them right back. Tante Marie didn't answer me, and I felt badly about what I had said. We rode the train in silence back to her house. When the train stopped, she motioned for me to follow her but she didn't say a word.

Inside Tante Marie's apartment, familiar faces greeted me.

Pictures of Uncle Ferdinand, my grandmother, and all my relatives who were present at their wedding. I picked up a little music box resting on a round, dark shiny table. I lifted the golden clasp when Tante Marie cut in, rousing me from my trance.

"Rosemarie, you must call your parents."

"One moment, Tante," I said.

I popped up the lid of the music box and stared, mesmerized. A little mermaid swayed from side to side on a rock, singing a German folksong I knew so well.

I don't know what it means that I'm so sad.
The story from long ago.
I can't forget the story from long ago.

It was a folksong written by Heinrich Heine, a German Jew, back in the 1800s. It is a song about a beautiful woman who guards the entrance to a harbor, luring sailors to shore with her beauty. Yet she is heartless. She knows about the violent waves and the jagged rocks on shore. The boats will crash, the vessels splinter, and lives and hopes will be dashed.

I wondered if the beautiful woman in that folksong wasn't Germany, the Germany that I knew that had seduced Jews for centuries with promises of religious freedom and prosperity, the nation that had drawn my own family to settle there a thousand years ago.

I stared at the mermaid. I couldn't bring myself to close the lid on her.

"Tante Marie, it's late," I said. "Shouldn't I wait until morning to call?"

"Rosemarie, I promised your parents you'd call tonight. They're so worried about you."

I closed the box carefully, followed Tante Marie to the phone next to her couch, and picked up the receiver. When the operator said hello, I asked her to connect me to my parents and gave her their number.

Vati answered. "So, you did it. You succeeded in leaving England."

"Yes, I did."

"It's not too late to go back."

"Yes it is," I said. "I have a one-week visa to Belgium and nowhere else to go. I can't go back to England, and we both know that Germany is out of the question. I've got to go to Africa."

I dug my fingers into the receiver and waited. I had not written about Herbert to my parents for a long time, other than to say that I didn't think I could get my visa. I knew they thought that was for the best, for they would have liked for our whole relationship to end as quickly as possible. I don't think they understood how attached I had become to this phantom below the equator.

"How can you even think of leaving us all to go to Africa to work for this ... stranger? How can your leave us and work for this man?"

I dug in my toes. "I love him."

"Love?" Father scoffed. "You have no idea what love is! You're only 18! It's puppy love! You have a crush on someone you don't even know."

"Uncle Phillip knows him."

"Uncle Phillip is crazy! Matching up an 18-year-old girl with a 30-year-old man in Africa. What was he thinking of? And, what will you live on? This doctor can't make a living. He's working in a jungle, and he's in absolutely no financial position to take care of you."

"But Vati, it's not Herbert's fault that he doesn't have much money. He'd love to have more patients, but patients won't come to him because he's German."

"That's his excuse, Rosemarie. He's no good and he's

137

covering up for himself. Don't throw your life away. Besides, you don't want to live in a place where you can die from the heat or malaria."

"But Vati, what can I do?"

"You have a waiting number to go to America. Stay in Belgium until it's called and then go with us. We'll go together and live with Margrit and Walter. We'll all be together again."

"I can't stay in Belgium."

"Yes you can! Don't worry so much about your visa. I have connections in the Belgian court, and I'll get it extended."

"Vati, I don't want to stay here. I want to go. Please trust me for once! I know that I'm doing the right thing. You just have to trust me. Please give me your blessing and say you will!"

There was a moment of silence and I then knew that the blessing would never come. "You do what you have to do, Rosemarie, but don't expect me to go against my conscience and give you my blessing. You are making the wrong choice and I am very unhappy with you."

The phone dropped against the chair in Bochum and then Mother picked it up. She was crying and was too distraught to speak.

"Rosemarie, please don't do this. What if we never see you again? I couldn't …."

There was the sound of weeping, and then my sister Heidi's voice. She had finished her photography classes in Berlin, and she said it was hard being the only child at home. "Mutti only talks about Margrit and the baby and Vati only talks about you."

"Bad things, I'm sure," I interjected.

"Rosemarie, he loves you. That's all. Don't go. Don't break up our family. It's hard enough as it is around here. All of our friends are gone, not to mention you and Margrit. We hear rumors about what the Nazis are doing to the Jews in Poland. It's a terrible time around here. Wait. I'll put Vati back on the phone. Tell him you're sorry and that you won't go."

Another moment of silence and another agonizing wait. Finally, my father came back onto the phone. "Rosemarie, you are under 21 and you will need my permission if you ever marry that man, and that is something I will never give you."

One tear rolled down my cheek, and then another. I hadn't thought about marrying Herbert, but still the words stung. Father slammed the phone down in Bochum and there was nothing to do but hang up the phone myself.

I peeled my fingers off the receiver. They were clammy and stiff, and my feet were leaden. I asked Tante Marie if she could show me to my bedroom. Tante Marie then answered something, but I didn't hear her. My eyes were no longer dry, and I mumbled something unintelligible and stared at the carpet as I carried my suitcase down the hall to the guest room. Then I turned without a hug or a kiss good-night and gently closed the door.

Inside, I stood there, with tears streaming down my face. Then I collapsed on the bed and sobbed as quietly as I could so Tante Marie wouldn't hear.

Yes, I cared about Herbert. Or, at least I thought I did. Yes, I wanted to see him. Actually, I couldn't wait to see him. But, I loved my parents and my family. When I was a child, I had never really disobeyed my father. Only once, when I refused to carry the flag of Imperial Germany to school on the Jewish holiday of Simchat Torah. Father wanted me to march around with the Imperial flag, and I wanted to parade with the one from the Weimar Republic. That was the only flag I knew, but my father was much more allegiant to the Germany he grew up with.

Now, I had gone against Father's wishes several times by writing to Herbert, getting a visa to Africa, and starting my trip. My father's words stung hard and he knew they would. He knew that deep down I needed his approval and that was one thing he'd never give me.

Still, what could I do? Where else could I go? To get a re-entry permit to England would take a month, even if the authorities would give me one. And, I only had a one-week pass to Belgium, and no possibility of going back to Germany without ending up in a concentration camp.

When the pillowcase on my pillow was soaked and I could cry no more, I sat up and opened my suitcase. There was a little ruffled pocket inside the suitcase, and I pulled out one of Herbert's letters for comfort:

15 September, 1939
My dear heart,

Soon we are going to be able to share all of our thoughts in person and I can hardly stand the waiting. Isn't it strange that this war – that separated so many men and women who loved each other – that this same war will bring us together?

You wrote to me from England that you are scared that we will never see our parents again. So let's make a promise to each other that we will do all in our power to have a reunion with your parents and mine and celebrate one day. Unfortunately, we are both aware that this lies in the distant future when the nightmare in Germany is over.

Herbert

CHAPTER TWENTY-TWO

Tante Marie

A FEW DAYS LATER, Tante Marie accompanied me to the airport but I didn't get past the Air France ticket counter, even with a ticket out of Europe.

"You cannot fly on this plane," said the Air France official.

"Why, monsieur?"

"Because, mademoiselle, you will be flying over France and it isn't safe. For all we know, you could be a German spy, taking pictures from the sky. No German nationals on this flight. Those are my orders."

But the J on my passport? I was a refugee, not a spy, I pleaded in French. "All I want is to go to Africa to work!"

The agent behind the ticket counter stared at the ceiling and drummed his fingers on the gray countertop. Only when I finished ranting away in French did he look me in the eye.

"I am sorry, mademoiselle, but those are my orders. And, if you do not like those orders, you can see the French consulate. Perhaps they will listen to your appeal."

At the French consulate in Brussels, I met the same resistance. I was German and a possible spy. There was no way that I could fly over France on my way to the Congo. Go away and don't bother us.

My transit visa in Brussels was good for just eight days, and I was desperate as the week progressed. Tante Marie said that there were ships sailing from Antwerp to Africa, so off I went to the Agence Maritime Belge, the Belgian shipping line. To this day, I don't know how I managed to get around Brussels and London and all those foreign metropolises that year. Yet I did, somehow. I was able to navigate myself to all the agencies and make myself understood with the little French I'd studied in school. Conjugating all those verbs for homework had helped.

Yet at Agence Belge, the agent laughed when I said I wanted to buy a ticket.

"Mademoiselle," he said. "Don't you realize that there is a war going on? Everybody is trying to go to Africa to work. We have no staterooms or berths available for six months. We are completely sold out!"

Sold out? Why, it could be months before I saw Herbert! "But sir, I've got to get out! Please, isn't there anything you can do? I'm desperate!" I cried.

The agent sighed. "Ah yes. Aren't we all… desperate. Let me guess. You cannot stay in Belgium any longer."

I nodded.

"You have a limited transit visa."

How did he know?

"Ah, the pangs of war. Well, in any case, I cannot help you. I am completely booked."

I had arrived in Brussels on the 14th of September and now it was the 20th. It was day seven and I needed to get out of the country by tomorrow, for when my eight-day visa expired the following evening, the Belgians could come after me. They could grab me by the arm, escort me to the German border, and dump me.

"But sir," I pleaded. "You must have … one seat."

"Not one, mademoiselle. Not today, tomorrow, or the following day. Not one for six months. Just like I said."

"Not one cancellation?"

"Nothing."

Slowly, I reeled and faced my fate. I pushed open the glass doors, eyes downcast and glum. I sat down on the steps outside the Maritime Agency because I had no idea what to do next or where to go. I wrapped my arms around my legs and rested my head on my knees. I had never prepared myself for what might happen if I wasn't able to use Herbert's plane ticket, because it never occurred to either of us that I might not. To be considered a potential spy? That was an unexpected twist.

I don't know how long I sat there, scrunched over on the steps, crying. An hour? A moment? Was it fleeting grief or an eternity in which I tried to envision where to turn? And yet soon there was salvation for I heard the shuffle of feet and the rustle of pant legs. Someone eased down beside me, hesitated, and then tenderly tapped my shoulder.

Looking up, I beheld the face of a young priest. He was wearing his black priest garb with the white collar and the sign of the cross. His skin was as soft as a child's, but his forehead was creased with an old man's concern. It was his eyes that haunted me, though. They were dark pools of tenderness and compassion, sunk in that baby face, filled with love and mercy.

"Mademoiselle, can I help you?"

I dabbed at my right eye and tried to clean up my tears. "Mon pere, I don't think so."

I tell you now: I don't know what came over me, but I told the priest my story. All of it, from the house I grew up in to my education in Switzerland and how I dressed up as a nun to come home. (His lips turned up ever so slightly into a smile on that one.)

I told him about the ninth of November, and the Gestapo's threats, and how I'd scrubbed floors for Mrs. Bathhurst to escape. I told him about Lilly and Rose, and about the man beckoning me to come work for him far away. I told him about the J stamped in my passport, and how hard it was to get exit visas and entrance visas when you were a Jew. Heaven help that priest, but I told him everything. And, unlike all the embassy people I'd encountered, the priest didn't blink or take his eyes off me as I reeled off my whole life story and my present tale. The priest's eyes were filled with emotion, and I knew this man was kind.

So there it was. My story.

"Quelle age as tu?" he asked me.

How old was I? I told him.

The priest shook his head. "Tu es tres jeune."

Yes, I was young, I suppose, but I don't think I was much younger than him.

"Tu es tres jeune d'etre seul." I was too young to be alone? Well, what about him?

The priest glanced away and stared out at the trees in the park across the street. I didn't know who this angel was or where he had come from, but he seemed like he wanted to help.

"Une moment," he said, excusing himself. "Je reviens."

I sat there and watched the priest walk down the street and disappear into the crowds passing along the boulevard. I was sure he would return, but unsure what he could do. How could the priest possibly help me?

Legs brushed past me and I watched the front and back of rain coats as men and women walked up the steps to the shipping company and down again. Finally, a half an hour later, just when I began to doubt that the priest was coming back, he returned. The priest's eyes were the same, deep sad depths of his soul, but this time he held something in his hand.

"Mon enfant," the priest began, sitting down next to me. "You have your whole life ahead of you. I am going to the Congo to serve my parish, but you are going to the Congo to save your life. If I get caught by the Germans, I don't think anything will happen to me. But, if you get caught by the Nazis, terrible things will happen. Do you understand?"

I nodded.

The priest extended his hand, and inside his right fist was a crumpled white ticket. A ticket from the Maritime Agence Belge.

I gasped. It was a ticket on the Leopold I, from Antwerp to Leopoldville, departing Antwerp tomorrow afternoon at 4 o'clock. I was speechless.

"Here, mon enfant, take my ticket," he said. "You can have it. You can take my place on the next boat, and God be with you."

Then the priest got up and hurriedly excused himself. "I must go," he said. "My parish is waiting."

I reached up and squeezed the priest's hand. "Merci, mon pere. Vous avez sauve ma vie." Thank you, father. You have saved my life.

Said the priest gently, "Va avec dieu." God be with me.

God's angel disappeared and I was left staring at a patch of black garb. I didn't know if I would ever see that priest again, but I was sure I could never forget him. I would always remember the depth of those benevolent eyes, and how that warm-hearted soul listened as I told my story.

The priest was gone and the only trace of the angel was his ticket in my hand. I got up slowly, and returned to Tante Marie's apartment to make a few last telephone calls.

It was Wednesday the 20th of September and I called Herbert's parents and told them that everything was set and that I was on my way to see their son. I had not seen them since February, although they had written me several times in England. Through their letters and Herbert's, I came to learn all about Herbert's past. How he was born in Berlin in 1908 to Hedwig Michaelson and Georg Moses. His father, Georg, was from East Prussia near the Polish border and made his living importing woven fabrics from England. Herbert's mother, who was from Berlin, taught school. While dissecting cadavers in medical school and learning about human anatomy, Herbert had decided to change his name from Moses to Molser -- to make it sound less Jewish. His parents, however, remained Mr. and Mrs. Moses.

"We were with you only a day, Rosemarie, but you won both our hearts," Mr. Moses said on the phone to me. "We really fell in love with you."

"Thank you, Mr. Moses."

Mr. Moses asked how my parents felt about my leaving, and I told him that they were still upset with me. "They don't know Herbert and they are afraid."

"Well, I will call your parents, sweetheart," Mr. Moses said, "because my wife and I understand how hard it is to let your child go so far away and for who knows how long. I will reassure your parents that our son is honorable and that he will take good care of their daughter. My wife and I have such a good feeling about the two of you, that this is meant to be and that everything will work out, that you will one day get married and live happily together forever. Our only wish is that we could be there to celebrate with you, for we would love to be with you and share your happiness!"

Through all the kind and reassuring words, I heard the sound of weeping. It had to be Mrs. Moses, for I knew how attached she was to her son. Herbert was the joy and light of her life. "Let me talk!" I heard Mrs. Moses say in the background, and Mr. Moses excused himself and handed the phone over to his wife.

"Oh sweetheart, I can't believe that such a young girl succeeded in leaving Germany and now England. What a brave little girl you are and how I admire your energy and courage! Finally, you are on your way and I am so proud of you! Proud and jealous because you're going to see my baby and I can't!"

There was the sound of scolding in the background and then a lonely soul weeping in the foreground.

"I'm sorry, Mrs. Moses," I said, cutting in. "I wish it wasn't so far away and that you could go there, too."

"From your mouth to God's ears," she said. "Good luck, sweetheart, and I know you're going to make each other very happy. I have to admire your endurance and bravery to go on this long trip and I will pray that you reach Africa without further difficulties. I hope God will reward you and my son with lots of happiness. And, I will thank God that you are going to be with Herbert so that now my child won't be alone anymore. Take good care of yourself and our only child and write to us as soon as you get to Africa."

"I will, Mrs. Moses!"

The next day, Tante Marie rode with me on the train from Brussels to Antwerp where I said my final good-byes to her. "Now go to your sister in New York if things don't work out," said Tante Marie, unsnapping the gold handle on her black leather pocketbook to retrieve her hankie and dab at her eyes.

"Dr. Molser is a good man and things will work out," I said.

"And if they don't?" said Tante Marie, patting her eyes with the hankie.

"Then I'll go to America, just like you said."

Tante Marie hugged me one last time. "Take good care of yourself, sweetheart," she said.

With the priest's ticket in hand, I boarded the Leopold I and sailed away from people I knew I loved to someone I thought I loved, and from the cobblestone streets of one continent to what would probably be dirt roads in another. I could remember reading what Herbert had written in a telegram after I'd written him about the useless airline ticket. "Everything's going to work out all right," he said. "Soon we will start our new life and I ask God that he bless your way. We're going to make it, sweetheart!"

CHAPTER TWENTY-THREE

Rosemarie

I **WAS SOON SICK** to my stomach and scared. The
Allies had mined the Gulf of Biscay to blow up German subs, and
there I was aboard the Leopold I, dipping in and out of those swells.
White caps reared, and I said a few prayers under the black veil of
my coat. My stomach churned along with the ship.

That evening, the white lights on the ocean liner stayed brightly
lit to identify us as a neutral ship, for this was war time and we
couldn't take a chance of being fired upon.

When you pass through the waters, I will be with you...

Mother Superior and the words of Isaiah were with me as
we cut through the choppy harbor and headed out to sea. Once
we were safely there and I got over my sea sickness, my spirits
stirred, for there were miles of blue water around me. I was sailing
in international waters and I was free. There would be no more

signs like the ones I had seen in downtown Bochum saying Juden Unerwunscht. I could buy food in any store, and there would be no sign telling me that I couldn't.

I shared a cabin with two sisters who were going back home. They were Belgian, and their father had accepted a job as an administrator in the diamond mines of the Congo. They had taken a holiday from the Congo to visit relative back in Belgium, and now they were returning home.

Renee was 23 and tall with long slender legs and brown hair that fell all the way to her waist. She had a relaxed and sporty look to her. Her sister, Ilona, was 21 and a little shorter and curvier with a mane of curly blonde hair. Ilona was paler than Renee, with freckles on her turned up nose.

"Did you see all those boys boarding the ship?" Renee asked, taking Ilona's hands in hers. "They kept looking at us because we are the only girls!"

"She's boy crazy," Ilona explained to me, tossing her curly hair back and laughing. "She has at least two or three boyfriends at a time! This ship load of boys is a dream come true!"

Renee pulled our window shade down, flipped on the light in our cabin, and unzipped her suitcase. She found just what she wanted on top, in a plastic bag. She lifted it up out of her suitcase, and a slinky red evening gown fell to the floor.

"I think I'll wear this tonight!"

Ilona rolled her eyes at me. "See what I mean? Those boys are in trouble already! Our ship is packed with Belgian men heading off to work in the Congo. They work with our father for three years to earn money, and then they take a six-month furlough. All that time alone makes them starved for a woman's attention. It's hard to get married when you're on a three year assignment away from home."

Ilona heaved her own suitcase onto a little bench at the side of our cabin and began unpacking her own gowns. "Get used to my sister, Rosemarie. Every time she wears that little red dress she has least one marriage proposal, and who knows how many more she'll have tonight. I pity all the boys on this boat!"

Renee hung her red dress on the back of the cabin door and turned to me. "Do you have any evening gowns to wear? If you don't, we could lend you one," she said.

"Oh, I do," I said, dragging my suitcase up and onto my bed. My mother had bought me two black velvet evening gowns before my trip to England. I pulled out one of them and heard both Renee and Ilona gasp. "Where did you get that from?" Renee demanded. "Oh my gosh, it's beautiful!" said Ilona. She turned the dress over and looked at the plunging back. Then she peeked around the back of the dress at Renee. "I think you've got competition!" she teased.

"Good!" Renee said. "I can't talk to three hundred men all by myself!"

We dressed for dinner in our evening gowns and then Renee sat me down on my bed and started applying some make up. I had never worn any make up before, and I was curious to see what I looked like after I'd closed my eyes and she'd applied eyeliner, mascara, rouge and lipstick.

I rubbed my lips together to spread the lipstick the way Renee showed me and then Ilona led me over to the bathroom mirror. "Look!" they both said.

"You're beautiful, darling!" said Renee.

"You should wear make-up more often!" said Ilona as I looked at an older reflection I didn't recognize. My eyes looked so much deeper and prettier with eye liner, and the bright red rouge and lipstick made me look more like an older movie star.

I drew my hands to my cheeks, dazed. What would my father think if he saw me wearing all this make-up? What would Herbert think?

Renee winked at Ilona. "I think she likes it!"

Renee, Ilona and I dressed up for dinner and dancing every night. Renee and Ilona would powder their cheeks in the bathroom with me, and the three of us would paint our lips red. With a hundred men for every woman, why not?

Those two weeks at sea are among my brightest memories. By day, I sipped a glass of Coca-Cola with Renee and Ilona on deck in the sunshine, laughing as the young men swooned around us. At night, lanterns twinkled magically and I danced with every boy who tapped me on the shoulder and asked. Even when the hands on my watch pointed to midnight, I kept dancing in the moonlight. If I was a newcomer at flirting, I made up for my inexperience in no time.

I was overcome by the beautiful French music crooning from the record player, such as the Soleil Arrendez Vous, which I remembered from school in Switzerland. The lyrics said that the sun had a rendezvous with the moon, which is what all of us young men and women had.

Herbert Molser?

I forgot all about him and why I was sailing in the first place. Subconsciously, I knew the day was coming when I'd be tied down with him, helping him build his practice. But I rested my head on the shoulders of my dancing partners and closed my eyes, pretending that there was no Herbert Molser in my life.

I swirled around the dance floor, with the tail of my evening gown and my conscience trailing behind. Young men gazed at me tenderly and I looked up at them adoringly.

My girlfriends and I barely slept. We'd giggle off to our cabins in the wee hours of the morning and chat about all the young men who begged to kiss us under the stars and the others who told us they loved us.

Meantime, the days grew more and more humid as the tropical sun began to beat down upon our ship. When we left, winter was on its way. But, as we crossed the equator and neared Africa, summer was just around the bend. Our cruise was three weeks long, and by the time the boat slipped into the harbor at Matadi, the capital of the Portugese colony of Angola, the three of us had each received half a dozen heated marriage proposals. Yet we tucked our memories away in our suitcases along with our evening gowns. We fanned ourselves and snapped our valises shut as the sun blazed.

We were here. Africa.

It was sweet and nauseating all at the same time. A half dozen African servants in white jackets fanned the deck with fronds, but people dripped with sweat all the same. Renee and Ilona and I dabbed at our temples with handkerchiefs and cried when we walked off the boat. We kissed each other on sweaty cheeks and said good bye through salty tears. We wrote our addresses down, but I didn't know if we'd really get a chance to see each other again. Then, Renee and Ilona pointed me toward the train to Leopoldville.

Fish sizzled in black pans where Africans cooked it alongside the street as I lugged my suitcases down the cobblestones.

I smelled unfamiliar fragrant spices, bananas hanging from the trees and pineapples in the field. White washed houses rose no higher than a second story behind protective fences. White women in long linen skirts bargained for what they needed in French, while African children ran barefoot down the streets, laughing in Kiswaheli.

When I arrived off the train in Leopoldville, I walked over to the hotel room I had reserved with Herbert's help and rested my bags at the foot of the bed. I splashed cold water on my cheeks to cool down, peeled a banana I had picked up at the registration desk downstairs, and settled onto my bed for a little nap. Lucky for me, French was the official language here and it was a language I knew well. I had two days to myself, and then I would need to ride a boat down the Congo River and complete my final journey.

A fan twirled on the ceiling of my room. No sooner did I close my eyes and try to catch a breeze when the telephone jolted me awake. I fumbled for the receiver. "Bonjour?"

"Welcome to Africa," a man said in German.

It was a deep voice I had never heard, but it belonged to a phantom I knew well. This was the voice of the man who had typed me letter after letter, wooing me with his hopes and dreams for a year. My heart fluttered. It had only been a few weeks since our last letters, and yet I felt like I was being gently caged.

My God, what have I done? Here was the voice of the man my parents begged me to forget in the place they urged me not to go. Why hadn't I listened? For now, hearing the voice of this man who wanted me, I knew there was no turning back.

"Oh Herbert, I'm scared!"

There was a moment of silence, a flash of his own hesitation, and then an attempt at reassurance. "Don't worry," he said. "Everything's going to work out all right. I love you."

Love? How could you love someone you'd never met? He didn't know me. And, for that matter, how could I have ever imagined I loved him? This .... stranger?

"How was your trip?" he asked politely.

Great. Tell him about all the marriage proposals, I thought.

"Oh, it was ... fine," I said, my heart starting to pound inside my rib cage. "It was ... long, but it went... fast."

I felt like I had betrayed someone, but I knew the men on the boat better than I did Herbert. I'd actually seen and talked to them!

"Did you bring your tropical helmet?"

"Yes, I bought one in England, just like you said."

"Well, be sure to wear it outside. The sun is a lot brighter down here than in Europe, and you'll need to protect yourself from the heat. Cover up your arms, too, because you don't want to get sun burned. It's going to take some getting used to this climate."

Mosquito netting covered my bed, and a tiny scorpion slithered at my feet. It was the first scorpion I'd ever seen in my life and I recoiled in horror.

"Are you okay?"

"Yes, I , I guess you're right. It'll take some getting used to."

There was an acknowledging pause on the other end of the phone. "Well, the whole trip up the river is going to be a very strange experience for you, because you're in the center of Africa. But don't be afraid. You'll grow to like it here."

Tears welled. "Herbert, I… I…. "

"Don't be scared," he said. "The worst is over. You're out of Europe and you're safe. Give yourself time to feel comfortable here. And, if you don't like it, you can leave. I told you – I won't stop you. You'll be free to go to your sister in America. But here you'll be my guest, and I just know you're going to fall in love with this place like I have."

"Time. I guess it just takes time."

"And don't be afraid about my feelings and think that I'm not happy with you, because I know I will be happy with you," he said.

The trouble was, I wasn't sure I could be happy with him. He sounded old and possessive, and felt so young – just like the priest had said.

My heart swirled like an overhead fan. I could feel the heat strangling me and sweat clamming my hands. It was cold up in Belgium but too hot for comfort down here. Much too hot. This unknown voice knew me too well and was making too many claims on my heart. What I offered before had been from a distance. Now, I was sweating out that commitment. My God. What had I done?

"I'm going to write you a letter every day and send it to every port," he said.

"But how will I get it?"

"The boat will dock each evening and it will be there, waiting for you."

"You haven't met me, and you could be very disappointed!"

"The greatest gift that you have given me is that you've trusted me," Herbert said, "and I hope that I can live up to that trust."

"I have trusted you no more or less than you have trusted me."

"You have come without anyone's encouragement and without anyone's help. When someone can cross the English Channel in the middle of a war like you did, then everything's going to be all right. And, your courage and determination have made such an impression on me. I know we are going to make it. I just know we will!"

"Oh, Herbert, I hope you're right! Promise me that if things don't work out…"

"Stop," the voice said. "There is no need for that. I have been so lonely in Africa and you have brought such a change to my life already, and I can't tell you how grateful I am that you made it possible for us to meet."

"But I didn't do it all by myself. You sent me the money and the ticket!"

"And it was worth every mark."

I placed the receiver back on the cradle and tapped absentmindedly, staring up at a cobweb, and then withdrew beneath the mosquito netting surrounding my bed. I lay there as the sun rose higher in the sky and scorched everyone outside in the street.

I twisted uncomfortably on my cot, staring at the tiny netting and longing for a comfortable breeze. Within minutes I was slipping out of my dress because it was too hot for clothes.

I had never experienced heat this smothering, and I didn't know if I could stand it. After months of trying to make this adventure happen, it was happening. What was it that mother used to tell me? Be careful what you wish for. I was caught in a net of my own weaving, and there was no turning back as far as I could see.

I slept for a few hours and walked into the lobby as the sun eased its way back down from the sky and the air mercifully cooled. Inside the hotel, ladies with pale, delicate shoulders sipped wine from goblets with stems as slender as their legs. They spoke French or Flemish and were as elegant as crystal.

Outside, the little African children played games throwing stones into the river, watching the crocodiles stir. Bare-chested ladies carried baskets on their heads and scolded them in Kiswaheli, a language as foreign to me as English had been.

In Germany, I had seen perhaps only one black man my entire life. Now the worn footpaths were full of them, selling African wares in their baskets. The men wore pants without tops, and there were gaps between their white teeth when they smiled. The ladies wore pieces of brightly colored cloth wrapped around their waists.

Inside the marketplace, there were baskets filled with ivory tusks for sale, and ebony elephant statues. I couldn't imagine how painful it must be for an elephant to have its tusks yanked off, or were the elephants killed and then robbed of their ivory?

It was all very new to me and totally fascinating.

The next day, I awoke after a fitful night's sleep, snapped my suitcases shut, and left the hotel. I gripped a handle with each hand, and walked across a black ramp onto an African river boat. The

Leopold I had been a true ocean liner like the Titanic, but the Reine Astrid was nothing but a clunker. It was white and musty-smelling, and it looked exactly like a river boat. African men and women filed onto the ship like cattle and settled among the chickens and wooden crates below. Chickens clucked below, and roosters crowed.

How was I ever going to get used to this colonial set up? In Germany, I had been discriminated against and treated differently from everyone else because I was Jewish, but here Herbert said whites were expected to treat blacks differently because of their skin color. Looking down upon someone as being inferior because of a matter of birth made no more sense to me here than back in Germany.

That evening, as I untied my silk bathrobe and hung it on a hook on the back of my door, I recalled all the girlish chatter with my Belgian roommates, and I realized how much I missed them. I pulled back the starched white cotton sheet and the thin pink blanket and fell asleep dreaming about our moonlit nights and conversations, dancing under the stars.

I woke up smiling, and then I reached up for my bathrobe and screamed. It was covered with little maggots. Silk worms. There was not much left of my bathrobe because they'd eaten it to shreds.

What was it that Herbert had said to me the night before? Welcome to Africa.

We traveled up the Congo River by day and stopped at a different port by night. Our journey would be ten days long until we reached Stanleyville, for the city where Herbert lived was deep in the heart of Africa. You couldn't be more dead center on the continent if you tried to point to the middle of a map with your finger.

"Why can't we travel at night?" I asked a waiter.

"Too many dangers, miss. Rapids, crocodiles and waterfalls."

Crocodiles. Only in Africa.

The arrival of our Congo River boat each evening at sundown was a source of excitement for the villagers, for when the boat docked every week, it brought food, mail and magazines. Coins for beggars as well. The villagers awaited us at each pier, and little naked African boys and girls held their knees to their chest and jumped, eager to dive for the coins that were tossed their way.

The water looked filthy. Garbage floated on top. A banana peel here, pieces of broken crate there, and probably raw sewage mixed in.

Yet mothers and daughters, grandmothers and aunts scrubbed their clothes on rocks at the side of the river and rinsed them in the river. Those who weren't washing their laundry sold fruits and vegetables at little stands, or African handiwork out of their baskets.

The evenings were at our leisure and we were free to stretch our legs and stroll the dirt road of the village and peek into the various baskets and huts. The place reeked of sweat. It was different from Bochum, Geneva, London, Brussels or any city I had ever known.

The shops were huts. Shanties as opposed to the well-heeled, established stores you'd find in Europe. In Bochum, you walked past brick and stone fronts that had stood for centuries. Here, I felt like I had traveled back at least a hundred years or more, to a time when streets were footpaths and people traveled by foot, cart or ox.

It was primitive, and the oppressive heat bore down on me till I felt like I would faint. Then I'd retreat to the boat and fan myself on my cot, begging for the evening thunderstorm that would cool things down for an hour.

Each day, my stomach knotted tighter and tighter as the boat eased gently through the canopied trees. The exotic birds flitted through the branches overhead and crocodiles skimmed the surface beside us while my stomach remained a burrowed knot of nerves.

I couldn't eat. My parents and everyone who had warned me about this trip were right. I was in Africa, in the jungle, and at the mercy of a stranger.

I had placed my trust in someone I could not see any more clearly than the bushes behind the trees.

One day I was sitting on the deck reading when a big black fly lit onto my arm with sheer veined wings and huge dark orbs. I shook my arm and screamed.

"What's the matter, young lady!" a man asked. He was wearing spectacles, and his hair was a salt-and-pepper gray. He looked wealthy, as he was dressed in a white collared shirt and white slacks.

I pointed to my arm. "A black fly bit me!" I said, pointing.

"Hopefully not a tsetse fly," the man said, shooing the fly away. Then he turned my arm over and rubbed it gently with his forefinger, looking for a puncture wound or welt.

"Whatever but it was, there's no sign of a bite, young lady. I think you're going to be okay."

I looked up at the man, horrified. "A tsetse fly!" I exclaimed. "Isn't that the fly that can kill you? The one who carries a parasite that can worm its way through your body and lead to a slow, agonizing death?"

The man peered over his spectacles at me. "That's the one, but there's really no sign of a bite," the man said. "My name's Frederick Spencer and I'm a doctor. You can call me Doctor Spencer."

Doctor Spencer pushed his glasses up on his nose and examined my arm again to see if there were any bite marks.

"Aha. Just fine and clean. No danger of tsetse flies or sleeping sickness here. You're more in danger of malaria, young lady. Tell me. Have you been taking your pills?"

"Pills?"

"Your quinine pills. For malaria."

"Oh yes, those pills. I have, sir."

"Well, the quinine is really what's most essential here. No need to worry about this."

"Thank God," I said. "I was so frightened. Everything is all so new and scary to me."

"It's too soon to tell, but how is your appetite? I mean, if you were in fact bitten by the tsetse fly, you'd be suffering from headaches and eventually you'd be too weak to eat."

"My appetite? Well, to tell you the truth, doctor, I haven't been able to eat much. This food is different from what I'm used to, and besides, I'm so scared and nervous about everything."

"I see." The doctor pushed the horn rimmed glasses up the bridge of his nose again. "Nervous? What's this all about? Is your family with you?

"I'm not traveling with my parents, doctor. I'm traveling alone."

The eyes blinked, yet the rest of the face was stone.

"Alone? What is a little girl like you doing on a ship like this up the Congo? This is no place for a young woman!"

"I ... I'm going to see ... a ... doctor I've been corresponding with. He invited me to come work for him."

The eyes blinked again and the face remained hard and taught. Not a muscle twitched.

"A doctor?"

This doctor waited for me to continue.

I explained everything as quickly and as best as I could.

"What on earth got into you to take such a gamble with your life!" Doctor Spencer said, his face reddening. "Going to see a strange man in this jungle, and relying on his word of honor! In the heart of the Congo, no less!"

"I...I've been corresponding with this doctor for some time now and he has been very good to me. He's been watching out for me, urging me to get out of Europe before the war broke out."

"Out of one inferno to another. Well, I don't trust any man who sends for an 18-year-old girl and pays for her trip." The doctor's legs were crossed, and his foot jerked up and down. I looked away and down at my lap, feeling sweat bead down my neck.

"That's very kind of you to worry about me, doctor, but I met this man's parents, and they were lovely people."

The doctor uncrossed his legs and leaned forward to speak, eye to eye. "Look," Doctor Spencer said, "When I get off this boat, I'm going to take a plane to Stanleyville. I own a hospital there, and I'm going to ask my staff about this Doctor Molser, this Moses of yours. And if I don't like what I hear, I'm going to pick you up myself and take you home to my family until I can arrange to get you safely back to your parents. I shall watch out for you like my own daughter. I have a daughter about your age and I would want some one like me to do the same for her. It is the most honorable thing I can do, to take care of you the way I would want my own daughter looked after."

"Thank you, doctor. I appreciate it, and I would be interested to hear whatever you learn about Dr. Molser. You are very kind."

Then, I excused myself quietly and retreated to my cabin. There I sat by the window and stared at the green forest lining the river banks as the boat slowly rippled past. Most of the landscape was a green virgin forest, tall, thick weeds and hanging trees. The riverbeds looked like walls, only the walls were made of plants and trees so thick that they might as well have been concrete. There didn't appear to be any way into that mess unless you had a machete.

No way out either, and I was scheduled to meet Herbert in five days.

CHAPTER TWENTY-FOUR

Rosemarie

IF YOU DON'T WANT TO get up in the morning,
you can spend the longest time tucked in your sheets. You can pass
an hour or two just thinking about what a boyfriend said, or how
much you miss him, or wondering whether he still cares. Then, when
you glance at your clock, you're shocked at how much time has
passed.

On the 25 of October, 1939, I was in no hurry to get out of
bed. When I finally did, I spent a long time in the bathtub and then
dressed with great care in a beige linen dress I had chosen. I knotted
the belt and brushed my hair over and over, studying myself in the
mirror, wondering what Herbert would see. *You're not that pretty
and he won't like you,* a voice said, staring at the blue-eyed girl in the
mirror.

Well, I'm not at all sure I'm going to like HIM, I retorted.

I finished packing, folding one side of my black velvet evening
dress and then pausing, fingering it tenderly, remembering how I'd

worn it dancing with the Belgian girls on the other ship. When would I have the chance to wear it down here? When would I have the chance to … dance?

I remembered the nights I twirled on a starry deck on the Leopold I. I glanced at the telegram I'd just received from Doctor Spencer, who had gotten off at a previous port. The telegram said his staff assured him that Herbert was a good man.

Good man or not, it was breakfast time and I had no desire to go to the dining room and eat. I wasn't hungry, and yet I had been unable to eat for days. I had lost at least five pounds. Maybe ten. My hip bones and collar bone were ridges on my skin.

There were so many mixed emotions gurgling within me. *Calm down,* I hissed. *You're acting like a little girl.* And yet, I was a girl.

Face the inevitable, I growled. And yet, I couldn't. The inevitable was an old doctor, and I was just 18.

They were right, all of them, I told myself, as I tucked Father's birthday poems and letters safely away in my suitcase and locked it. *He's too old for you. Why didn't you listen?*

I paced up and down in my cabin. Then, around the deck near my suitcases. Left foot. Right foot. Trudge. Trudge. Stare.

If I could, I would have sailed back to Tante Marie and Uncle Phillip and begged them to take me in. I wanted my mother and father, Margrit and Heidi.

I awaited my fate alongside my valises and leaned against the railing for support. Waves softly rippled below as the boat neared the wharf at Stanleyville where Herbert lived. A couple of people standing beside me on deck were returning to Stanleyville and knew Herbert. They said they'd point him out to me.

We rounded a bend and slipped through canopied trees and there was the village. Unlike the last few ports, there were no naked African children jumping in the river, and it looked cleaner. The wharf was paved, an improvement over the worn dirt path that served as the last pier.

Though the wharf and streets were paved, Stanleyville was still less developed than Leopoldville, and unlike any city I'd ever seen in my life. It was a colonial city on a frontier, and the squat little buildings were bleached white. Back in Bochum or London, the buildings were taller and browner and more often brick. Back home, there were elegant department stores and smaller ones, selling books, antiques or hats ... anything you could imagine. Here, I saw less refined venues. Women wore colorful scarves on their heads selling chicken, fruit and vegetables out of coarse baskets in open-air stalls. There was the smell of pineapple and mango in the air. We eased alongside the pier and dropped anchor. There were so many onlookers standing and watching us - men in seersucker suits, and women in sleeveless frocks and high heeled shoes and pearls. A brunette in a pale yellow linen shirt dress with long wavy hair was clutching a white patent leather pocketbook and craning her neck to see us getting off the ship. There was a group of three men standing together alongside her. One in pale blue pants and a white button-down shirt rolled up to the elbows was smoking a cigarette, waiting.

Which one of the men was Herbert? How would I recognize him? I had seen pictures of Herbert at his parents' house in Berlin, and he had mailed me additional photographs. Still, would I be able to recognize him in a crowd?

I turned around to look behind me on the ship, searching for the people who said they knew Herbert and would point him out to me. There were so many people jostling me forward that I couldn't find them. I scanned the gentlemen smiling and waving on shore and tried to picture Herbert's photograph. Was that one Herbert? Or, that one a couple of heads away?

I'm sure I will find you, Herbert had written me. *Those last few minutes are going to be very painful for both of us when we finally meet, but we have all our lives to make up for it.*

It was time to move. White people always disembark a ship first before the native Africans, and passengers were surging toward the plank, jostling me forward. I had to get off the boat whether I liked it or not. I couldn't think about the blacks who would have to follow me because they weren't good enough to walk beside me.

I didn't want to think about them either. It reminded me that my father wasn't as perfect as I thought he was. My father had his own prejudices, and his were against Polish Jews. He treated his Polish clients no better than the blacks on this ship. He kept the men in shabby suits and yarmulkes waiting in a separate room where the end tables were a little less polished and the sofa fabric a little more tattered and worn. These Jews weren't allowed to mingle with my father's German clients.

I turned my eyes. How many months had I been writing Herbert? How long had I so desperately fought for a visa to come here? Now that we were finally going to meet, I wanted to run to the back of the boat and throw up.

A man tapped me on the arm as I began walking down the plank. Startled, I looked up. It was one of the passengers who said he had known Herbert. He spoke to me in French and pointed toward the dock. Did I see that man standing there, the professional looking man in the pressed blue and white seersucker suit with the white collar and blue tie? "C'est le docteur Molser," the passenger said.

Le docteur Molser seemed to be staring right at me through his circular horn-rimmed glasses, as if he knew right away it was me. Herbert was not as tall as I had imagined him, and his hair was darker than I had pictured.

There was a serious look to Herbert. The corner of his lips

turned down just like his mother's, and he looked too dull for my liking. Too humorless. Herbert was too …everything. And, he was not what I had pictured all this time.

I didn't want to take another step forward, yet I couldn't take a step back.

The sun was scorching my cheeks and nose, and I could feel the sweat soaking through the back of my dress. Oh God, what have I done? I raised my hand to wave back to Herbert but twisted it behind me and rubbed the back of my neck instead. My heart was somewhere in the pit of my stomach, yet Herbert continued to beckon and wave. What had he written in his last letter?

My golden girl,

This is the last time that I have to write you. I see many boats come and go at the harbor and I can hardly stand it knowing one of the next ones will be yours! Soon we'll be together and we'll be able to share all of our thoughts and feelings in person. The time is so close and it is more excitement that I can bear.

That man over there wrote… that? My legs barely carried me off the boat. Slowly, I made my way down the ramp, or was it an altar? A marriage altar? A sacrificial altar? My desire to continue faltered along with my footsteps. A once lovesick heart pounded as it came face to face with what it had pined for and I crept closer to my final destination - the man I had dreamed of, in the place I had fought so hard to come to, there just a few steps away.

Him?

I stepped onto the pier reluctantly. Herbert ran forward to greet me holding a beige tropical helmet in his hands.

"Rosemarie?"

A second elapsed as I pondered. Did I have to admit it?

I nodded.

"Willkommen zu Afrika," Herbert said in German, and then placed his helmet back on his head.

Welcome to Africa.

Here was the face and voice of my poet.

I looked down at my watch. 10 a.m.

Herbert was about an inch shorter than me. He wasn't Gert's height, nor did he have Gert's broad chest or his shy smile, Gert's once youthful, boyish smile.

What was it that had struck me when I met Herbert's parents in Berlin? Oh, that I stood a fraction of an inch taller than them. That was it.

Herbert reached up to kiss me hello on my cheek.

I turned my head. I didn't want to kiss a stranger.

Herbert appeared startled, but straightened his shoulders and bore himself up proudly. He was wearing one of those seersucker suits that the wealthy fathers used to wear at the beach during our summer vacations in Europe. Herbert reached across the emotional divide for my hand.

I recoiled.

"Make sure you put your helmet on," Herbert said, regaining his composure. "The sun is a little strong now."

I obediently placed my helmet on my head and tugged it down over my eyes so I couldn't see Herbert and he couldn't see me. I glanced down at my watch again, wondering what my parents were doing.

Herbert leaned over to pick up my suitcases. "Komm wir gehen zu neineim auto,"

Come on," he said. *"I'll show you to my car."*

I turned to look back at the boat. If I ran, I might be able to clamor up the gangway and beg the captain to take me back to

Leopoldville. Of course, I didn't have any money for a return ticket. And, I had no idea what I would do next.

So, I followed a man's heels, and stared at the back of a bunch of stripes on Herbert's suit. I felt like I was wearing them. Prison stripes.

Herbert turned, drew up the corner of his lips, and waited for me to catch up.

"I feel funny with you walking behind me," he said. "Are you okay?"

Grudgingly I came closer.

"That long trip up the river must have been terrible for you, but it has come to an end now," he said.

I nodded.

Herbert stabbed at the awkward silence as we neared the parking lot. "I'm so happy that you are all right because I was terribly worried about your passage from Antwerp. I was worried about your sailing in the middle of a war, but I felt better when the German diplomat reassured me that the neutral ships would be safe."

Remember all that praying I did that we'd sail through the Bay of Biscay without hitting any mines? Well, I wish we had hit one.

Finally we reached Herbert's car. He set down my suitcases in back of a little green Oldsmobile convertible and fumbled in his pockets. Keys jangled, and then he unlocked a tiny trunk and set one of my bags inside. Herbert placed the other in the back seat.

"This is my car. I hope you like it." Herbert said with a nervous smile.

Like it? I thought the car was awful. A hideous color and a uselessly tiny interior.

I wondered what would happen if I screamed and pretended that Herbert was kidnapping me against my will. Would I be able to get out of my predicament? Herbert sat down next to me in

169

the driver's seat and reached for my hand. "We have to talk about things," he said.

A lady in a navy blue dress and pointed heels tottered over and waved a white gloved hand. "Oh, Docteur Molser, Docteur Molser!" she called in a French accent.

Herbert withdrew his hand from mine and looked up at her as she ran over to his side of the car. The blonde-haired woman with the bouffant hair arched her pencil-thin eyebrows at me, but did not inquire who I was. Instead, she covered her chest with the palm of a glove and said apologetically in French, "Dr. Molser, can I bring my little girl over to you this afternoon? She has a sore throat."

I understood every word, and was amazed at how much French I remembered from Switzerland and Belgium. "Mrs. Swenson, I am so sorry your daughter is not feeling well. I will be happy to see her after I get married. Perhaps you could bring her later on this afternoon?"

Herbert was getting married? To whom?

I pushed the car door open, tumbled out onto the pavement and fainted.

CHAPTER TWENTY-FIVE

Herbert

HERBERT DABBED AT A SCRAPE on my
forehead with a wet handkerchief.

"I don't think you banged your head too hard, but it's probably
going to be swollen for a few days," he said. "Come on. Let's get you
back in the car and go home."

I squirmed and scrunched against the side of the car and
heard the haunting echoes of my own words: Promise me if you're
disappointed we'll call the whole thing off. Better a quick end than a
horrible thing without ending.

I felt a gentle touch on my arm.

"Did you get my letters?"

"Which letters?"

"The ones I sent you at every port."

I turned to face him. "I didn't get any letters."

There was a sea of emotion in Herbert's dark brown eyes and he looked very upset.

"I had a feeling this was going to happen. We need to talk," he said and sighed. "I don't want you to be scared about the whole thing, but we are going to have to get married today."

"I'm not getting married to you," I said. "I don't even know you."

"Foreign women entering the Congo must now prove that they are financially independent or show a return visa to Europe. You must marry me or be deported back to Germany."

"Deported?"

"Yes, and the timing is working against us. Normally you would have 48 hours, but since today is Friday and the government offices are closing for the weekend, you have to marry me now."

I stared at Herbert coldly. "You said we could try things out. That I could work for you for awhile and see how I liked it here."

"I had no idea that the time we had to get to know each other would be cut so short. The problem is your reentry permit to England. I tried to get a dispensation but couldn't."

"You said I could see what I thought of this place. Whether I liked it enough to stay. You didn't tell me I had to marry you."

"Rosemarie, I didn't know…"

"You're lying," I said, my voice rising. "My family was right. You had ulterior motives and you lied to me."

"I didn't lie to you," Herbert said, turning his eyes toward mine. "I would never lie to anyone, and you can be sure I would never do it to someone who is so close to me."

"Yes, you did lie to me," I said, starting to cry, "and you can take me right back to the dock. I'm not getting married to you. I don't even think I like you."

Herbert pressed his lips tightly together. "You have got to trust me," he said. "You can be sure that I have never said anything that wasn't true."

I stared off at the palm trees in the distance, tears trickling down my cheeks. Father told me not to come here. Mother said I was too young and that I was ruining the rest of my life. God my parents were so right. How was I going to marry this man in this faraway jungle when I didn't even like the looks of him?

"You are a very brave girl and I respect all that you did to get out of Europe and make your trip here. I was really looking forward to your coming and wanted everything to work out just as you hoped. I'm sorry that the laws did not make this possible."

"Well you could have told me!"

"I didn't know. The war changed everything."

"It's a good thing your letter never arrived to tell me I had to marry you or I would have drowned myself in the Congo."

"Rosemarie, it isn't that bad…"

"Not that bad? What are you talking about? What could possibly be worse?"

I regretted it as soon as I said it. Herbert fingered his keys with a faraway look in his eyes. Maybe he heard echoes of our letters. I know I did.

"You know, my dearest heart, the first day of our meeting will be in our memory as the most beautiful day in our lives."

We drove past palm trees, mango trees and white stucco buildings. I turned to look at Herbert who was staring straight ahead. "I don't want to get married," I said.

"I know you don't," Herbert said, with his eyes still focused on the road. "It's just that you have no choice. I wanted to prepare you, but unfortunately my letters didn't reach you. Now you've got to trust me and understand that I am telling you the truth, that unfortunately, right now, you have no choice but to marry me."

Tears fell on my lap. "No choice at all?"

Herbert shook his head.

There's no way out, I thought. No way out and I've got to…

"Everything will work out all right," Herbert said, pulling in front of his little stone house on Rue du Bois about 15 minutes later. He opened the trunk of the car and removed my suitcases. Then, he helped me out of the car and introduced me to his African housekeeper Ferdinand. I smiled at Ferdinand and reached out to shake his hand, but Ferdinand's eyebrows burrowed closer together, and he looked at me puzzledly. His hand remained where it was, on the handle of one of my bags.

Herbert rushed in and took my hand instead. "It's okay, Rosemarie," he said. "He knows you're happy to meet him." I looked at Herbert's anxious eyes and then up at Ferdinand, who had ignored me and was walking toward the house carrying two of my suitcases. What was going on? What had I done wrong?

Herbert led me by the arm up the short flagstone walk to his house. "Rosemarie, I think you should lie down for a few minutes and rest," he said. "I know this isn't what you wanted, but I've got to arrange a few last things for the marriage ceremony. It's going to be all right."

I followed my suitcases into Herbert's living room. Inside, I saw all the furniture he had described in his letters, just the way he had pictured. There was the living room couch, covered in red, brown and yellow stripes, and there was Herbert's steel desk with his black typewriter on it, the one he used to woo me here.

There were two brown upholstered chairs in the living room, and a dark narrow coffee table. Herbert led me into a bedroom and set down my suitcases.

"This is where you can sleep," he said, adjusting my suitcases neatly in front of a four-poster dark cherry bed. "Why don't you rest from your trip and take your time getting ready." Then he walked out and closed the door gently behind him.

I stood there for a moment, breathing hard, and then I walked over to the door and locked it, leaning my head against it. After taking a couple of very deep breaths, I sat on the floor of the bedroom, opened up my trunk, and hugged my knees.

I was young and Herbert was old. I had dreamed of him for months and I had been imagining the wrong guy. This one was too short and too unattractive, not to mention old.

It didn't matter what plans I had in life because life always made other ones for me and I had to go along with them. I'd done it, too. Hadn't I? I'd gone away to school in Switzerland, come back home when my parents' money ran out, and then advertised myself as a maid and moved to a country where I didn't know the language. I'd learned how to cook and learned how to speak English. I'd adjusted to all of it.

Only this was too permanent. But, what choice did I have? Where could I go, and where could I run? I couldn't go back to Germany and I didn't have enough money to go to America. Besides, what was in America? Walter was ill and Margrit was struggling and working two jobs. Life was not paradise there.

I unzipped my suitcase and reached inside to flip through the layers of clothing I'd packed with so much hope and elation. What do you wear to a wedding you didn't anticipate? I chose a beige silk dress with short sleeves that Mrs. Hirschberg had made for me back in Bochum. I lifted it out, smoothed out the wrinkles and then zipped it on. I braided my hair because it was too hot to hang loose, all the while wishing I could climb up the side of the house like a salamander and disappear into a tree.

At 4 o'clock I stood beside Herbert and two of his friends, Mr.

Meyer and Mr. Rothschild, in front of the Mayor of Stanleyville at the Ministere des Colony. The mayor mumbled the ceremony in French, and the time came to say our vows.

"Oui," Herbert said out loud. Then he leaned over to whisper something in my ear. "I love you," he said. "I have from your very first letter. We are going to have a beautiful life together. Trust me."

It was now my turn to agree to this union. Herbert nudged my chin up to face the judge. "Oui," I whispered. Then the dam on my emotions broke as he placed a gold band on my finger, and my cheeks were awash in tears.

Herbert turned his head to kiss me, with a look of both longing, love and concern. Now I had the chance to make that dream of kissing him come true. Instead, I turned and wiped the tears from my eyes.

I locked myself in Herbert's bathroom while my new husband and his two old friends drank champagne in the kitchen. I'm sure Mr. Meyer and Mr. Rothschild were wondering why the bride was behaving so strangely, because the reception didn't last long. I heard the clink of glasses, a few "Au Revoirs," and then a gentle knock on the door.

"Komm," a voice said. "Ich muss mit wDir sprechen." He wanted to talk to me.

I stayed where I was, crouched on the floor.

"You have nothing to fear," Herbert said. "You can come out when you want to. I understand why you are upset, and I apologize for what I did, but I had no choice. Yet, I understand how you feel, being forced to marry someone you hardly know. You can stay in there as long as you want, but maybe you'd like to come out and take a walk."

I twisted the gold ring on my finger, the one Herbert placed there just an hour ago. I never imagined I would miss Europe so much, or my parents. I even missed America, even though I'd never seen it, because that was where Margrit was.

"Rosemarie?"

I twisted the golden ring around and around my finger, longing for the people who loved me, the people I always took for granted would one day be at my wedding. Who thinks they're going to marry a stranger, in front of strangers?

"All right," he said through the door. "Take your time and think things through. I would love to see the sunset with you, but you can come out when you want to and use my room. The mosquito netting will protect you while you sleep. I'll sleep on the couch in the living room."

There was a small square window over the bathtub, a strange looking thing since there was no glass pane. It was just a square opening closed by a pair of wooden shutters, and I stepped into the bathtub, pushed the shutters open, and looked outside. Above me, there were stars and constellations I had never seen before in Europe, and Ferdinand squatted and cooked dinner over an open fire outside his hut in front of me. I could smell the wood burning and see him tearing off manioc leaves and placing them in the kettle on the fire beneath the banana tree in the back yard. Manioc was a leafy shrub, Herbert had said, and Ferdinand often boiled the leaves or roots for dinner. Herbert thought it was tasteless, like flour.

Suddenly, I felt water splattering against my nose and hands. Soon, sheets of rain hailed down everywhere, shooting up clods of mud. Ferdinand hurriedly carried the kettle inside and I curled up in the bathtub, silk dress and all. I rested my head on my knees. I don't know how long I was lost in thought when I looked up and beheld blanketing darkness and heard the rustling of leaves.

Outside, an indigene – a native African - with gray curly hair wisping around his earlobes, poked in the flowers and weeds growing along the house. He was carrying a flashlight in his left hand and a machete in his right, and his dark silhouette could be seen clearly in the deepening shadows. I ducked and let him pass.

Herbert wrote that he had once been sitting in this very bathroom when a deadly Viper reared its head and stared him in the eye. Herbert then took the advice of his European friends and hired one of the natives to prowl for snakes while he slept safely.

Herbert said that I could sleep in his bedroom. I took him up on it and ran.

CHAPTER TWENTY-SIX

MORNING LIGHT FILTERED through the mosquito netting but I closed my eyes. What was the point in getting up today or tomorrow? The mosquito netting surrounding the bed looked like a shroud. Herbert was out there in that living room and my life was over. What was I thinking dreaming of Herbert all those months and coming here? I kicked off the sheet angrily. It was so hot here and the sun was still rising.

I turned over onto my stomach and buried my face into the mattress and then flipped over again. Finally I couldn't bear it. I needed air, even if it meant seeing him.

There was a pair of knee-length shorts in my suitcase. I zipped them up and slipped out of the bedroom and past a glass and aluminum table in the living room. My eyes focused on the rug so I wouldn't have to face him. I could see him, though, out of the corner of my eye. He was sitting by himself at the table. I could see his

Erika typewriter on the desk in back of him, and the glass of juice in front of him on the table. I didn't know what to say, but neither, it seemed, did he. I pushed open the screen door and let it bang behind me.

Where could I go besides the porch? If I knew the way to the village I would have run there. It faced the river and maybe I could drown myself. Maybe I could feed myself to the crocodiles.

I found a wicker rocking chair out on the veranda and sat back, closing my eyes and feeling my chest press against my heart and the skin tighten around my neck. I rocked back and forth, wanting to go home, dreaming of home.

It had been ten months since I'd been back home with my mother and father in that beautiful stone house in Bochum, where my mother set the table with white linen for dinner and we all talked about books, politics, and the latest letters we'd received from our relatives, like Tante Johanna, my mother's sister, or Tante Kathe, my father's sister. Tante Johanna lived in Frankfurt and Tante Kathe in New York.

I pitched forward and back in the rocker, a little quicker now. My home was in Germany, wasn't it? And yet, what about all those signs on the park benches?

Nicht Fur Juden. Not for Jews.

Margrit was in America and there were no signs on the benches there, but would America feel like home, the way I remembered home? Margrit was struggling and barely had time to write, now that Walter was sick and there was no one else to pay the rent or buy my parents a boat ticket to America.

I had no idea where home was anymore, but I was sure of one thing. It wasn't here. Not with Herbert, and not in this strange place. I felt my nerves begin to prickle in the heat. It was too hot here. My father had warned me that I was ruining my life coming here and he was right. What did Herbert mean when he said I could come and work for him? Doing what? Father had warned me that Herbert was giving a false impression of his life and I could hear him saying, "I told you so." Herbert said that he started work at 7 o'clock in the morning and didn't finish until 9 o'clock at night, but I hadn't seen any patients besides the woman at the wharf. This did not seem like much of a practice, although it was Saturday.

Where could I go and what could I do? Returning to England or the Harrisons was impossible because I didn't have a reentry permit, and even if I wanted to go to America, I'd still have to wait until my number was called back in Germany. That was the way it worked. You were granted a visa based on your homeland, and Germany was still my place of birth. Then, even if my number was miraculously called in Stuttgart, how could I buy a boat ticket? I had spent everything I had to leave Europe and now I had nothing left. Not one franc in my purse, and what could I do to earn one? I couldn't be a domestic or nanny down here. I could do that in England but not here. Hardly anyone employed a white or European housekeeper. The children were taken care of by black women.

It was too hot to rock any faster. I was slowing down when I saw a trunk rounding the corner, and then a pair of dark eyes and long floppy ears. A parade of elephants began clumping down the street in front of me, corralled by two native indigenes with skin the color of dark chocolate. The elephants carried stacks of lumber on their gray wrinkled backs, and they curled their trunks up toward the seamless blue sky while plodding down the street.

I stopped rocking altogether and froze. I had never seen elephants in Europe, and these animals had a look of resignation in their dark eyes, chained to their fate.

I watched them pass, my eyes unexpectedly tearing. I had

to make the best of this, even if Herbert was duller than I had ever imagined. Margrit was wearing herself out in America, food was being rationed back in Germany, and I would have my own challenges here. Maybe I could just avoid Herbert, for months if I needed to. I could be civil, but live by myself in this house until I figured out a way home.

CHAPTER TWENTY-SEVEN

ONE OF MY MOTHER'S MORNING chores
back in Germany was to accompany our cook to the marketplace,
planning the mid-day meal and shopping for the ingredients
that our cook needed for dinner. The cook would bounce along
behind my mother, carrying a big wicker basket. Sometimes, I
had accompanied them both downtown to Wilhelmplatz, to the
market surrounded by the district court, the local court, and Father's
office. At the front of official buildings in the marketplace, I would
point out the fresh cherries, strawberries or blueberries I wanted
my mother to buy for me. Asparagus in May, strawberries in June,
peaches and plums at the end of July, and pears and apples in the
fall. We'd fill up the basket and then discuss dinner all the way
home.

On Monday, at breakfast, Herbert asked if I'd like to go into
town and shop with Ferdinand. I nodded my head without looking

up at him. I was bored of hiding out in the bedroom, and I wanted to know how to walk to town so I could escape there by myself.

It was only a short distance to the center of town, Herbert said, and I followed Ferdinand while Herbert began seeing his patients. As the sun roasted the tip of my nose, I remembered something Herbert had said in one of his letters. "If one has to walk, one feels being in the tropics."

An African woman approached us on the sidewalk, carrying one basket on her head and another in her arms. She continued walking on the sidewalk as Ferdinand passed her, but when I neared, she stepped down from the curb and into the street. I tried to smile at the woman, but she walked with her head bowed and her eyes focused on her bare toes. She passed me and then stepped back up onto the sidewalk and kept on walking.

There was such a separation between black and white in this country that I couldn't get used to, I didn't feel any better about myself because my skin was white, nor could I understand that feeling in others. It was wrong to treat another class as being less worthy than you. "That's because you're a good person," Herbert once wrote. "You're the kind of girl who would shake an African hand as if it was a white hand, and hug an African baby as if it was your own."

The smell of pungent spices wafted toward me as I neared the marketplace. There were about two dozen stalls crowded together, and an African or Indian merchant stood inside. Sometimes, the stall was just a long table, wide enough to sell wares, and sometimes the stalls were clusters of tall baskets with food or crafts inside. I heard the sound of French. Bonjour! Kiswaheli. Yambosana. Good day to you. I smelled hot peppers and heard carp sizzling in pans. I saw other fish drying in tin pans.

Merchants stood quietly, waiting for me to buy. Besides

fish, there were papayas, sweet, succulent mangoes, and stacks of pineapples, fresh and ripe. There were piles of vegetables I had never seen before.

The back of my dress was damp with sweat, even though I had been outside for less than an hour. I saw a woman wrapped in a large hot pink scarf with white swirls and a matching bandanna around her head selling flowers. "Yambo," I said, nearly curtsying before I straightened up, remembering how I had offended Ferdinand. The women smiled at me and I saw her teeth, white as salt but with gaps in the top row. The woman pointed to exotic colored flowers that I had never seen before in Europe, but I shook my head. I didn't know what I'd do with the flowers, and besides, I had no money.

I spotted Ferdinand examining pineapples not far away from me. He held up pineapples one by one, turning them around to look at them. Then he set down two of them in front of him on the pile of fruit and reached into his pocket.

Chickens squawked in this marketplace, piquing my interest. Suddenly I found Ferdinand at my side, pineapples in a bag, and the shop owner looked expectantly at the two of us.

Ferdinand's eyes were intent on the chickens bobbing around in a pen, and he pointed to one of them. He spoke in Kiswaheli, and he must have said, "I want that one," because the merchant chased after a brown chicken which scooted off and tried to outrun him but couldn't. The shopkeeper lunged and grabbed the chicken, holding it up by its squirming neck. Wings flapped in desperation but the shopkeeper handed the chicken to Ferdinand who set down his pineapples and grabbed it by the legs.

A live chicken? Not at our meat market, and I turned my nose aside. My mother's chickens arrived plucked and quartered from the butcher.

How different it was here. I looked up at the sky and prayed for the war to end and for the day when I could leave here and go home, wherever my parents were. I wanted everything to be as it was, before 1933 and away from this jungle with its thick green brush and the smell of body odor, pepper and fish.

When I returned to Herbert's house, I didn't want to go in. Then, I told myself I could go inside but not talk. I didn't have to speak to him, did I?

CHAPTER TWENTY-EIGHT

At FIRST, I WOULDN'T EAT any meals with him. Then, I relented. Neither one of us felt much like eating though. Herbert looked sad, sipping his juice and then fingering his napkin in his lap. I nervously twisted my own napkin in my lap, wringing the ends rather than eating a piece of fruit or breaking off a piece of fresh bread that Ferdinand had baked.

After breakfast, I would rock on the veranda, reading a book. When Ferdinand went shopping, I accompanied him because it gave me a chance to flee. Then, when we returned and I could feel the sweat on my body, I filled up the bathtub and soaked.

On the Friday following our wedding, Herbert said, "The boat is coming in today. It's bringing the weekly mail. Would you like to go?"

Letters only came once a week by ship and I was hoping for a letter from home. I couldn't wait to see the familiar handwriting of my parents or sisters, and to see the return addresses I knew well.

"Yes," I said quietly.

Herbert drove me to the same pier where we had met, while I tried to sit as far away from him as I could on the front seat. There, we waited at the wharf, near the same dock where I'd first seen Herbert.

A ship steward called our names and we raised our hands and stepped forward to accept our mail. There was a little bundle, with my letters on top of Herbert's letters and a few medical and scientific magazines.

There were letters from my mother, father and Heidi, and my lips curled up happily at the sight of my name in their handwriting. I ripped open the envelopes in Herbert's car while he set his letters and magazines on the front seat between us.

17 October 1939. My dear Rosemarie, I'm thinking of you out on the ocean, and I admire your courage and how you took your life in your own hands. You are so young and all life with its valleys and its mountains is ahead of you.

Deine Mutti

My father scribbled a note to me on the back, so that he wouldn't have to use a new piece of tissue paper, saving weight and postage. *When you receive this letter, the trip will already be behind you. So this will be our welcome, and we wish you with all our heart that your long trip brings you happiness and that all your wishes will be fulfilled. Say hello to Dr. Molser and tell him that he has to have a lot of understanding for our doubts about letting you go so far away. Those doubts were out of our love for you, and I hug you with the wish that it is a happy journey.*

Dein Vati

I stared at my father's beautiful handwriting, unable to fold up the letter and tuck it neatly back in its envelope as I usually did. How could I send my family a telegram and tell them the news, that Herbert and I had done what they cautioned me against. We'd gotten married.

We try to live normally, Heidi wrote. Our plans to leave Germany are advancing very slowly and our waiting number in Stuttgart is still a little ways off. We haven't heard from Costa Rica or Bolivia and we were seriously considering going there. Margrit wrote us about Mexico and maybe we can do something about that.

I'm still hoping they're going to call our number in Stuttgart. I hear from everybody that affidavits are becoming more difficult and that there are difficulties paying for the passage to America, and I don't know if Margrit and Walter have enough money to help us. But, I'm full of hope that we'll still get out of here.

I felt a solitary tear run down my cheek when I looked across the seat to see Herbert, sitting there, watching me. One hand was on the steering wheel and the other was on the key in the ignition. Herbert's eyes were filled with concern. "Is everything all right?" he asked.

I had been avoiding Herbert as much as possible, and now, for the first time, the worried look on his face made me feel guilty. This marriage had to be as difficult for him as it was for me. Imagine marrying a teenager who acted like a teenager and wanted nothing to do with you, who slipped out of the house every chance she got and hid behind the closed door of her bedroom. Surely this wasn't what Herbert had bargained for after all those letters and all those months of waiting. I had to be a disappointment as much as he was to me.

If there was one gift I had, it was the ability to see the world through other people's eyes, to understand how they were feeling. Herbert had been all alone in Africa longer than I had, and he had been looking forward to seeing me. Herbert missed his parents as much as I did. We were both orphans until this war was over, or until our parents could join us.

"I'm fine," I said. "Really I am."

I knew he was too smart to believe me. "Do you want to talk about it?" he asked.

I shook my head.

That evening, Herbert invited me to watch the sun set with him and I agreed. He had shown that he cared about me. Besides, what did I have to do that evening? I was growing tired of being by myself.

We returned to the river front, and my eyes were captivated and I forgot all about how uncomfortable I was as I watched an orange ball dip into the muddy Congo River. When the sun dissolved into the river, the reddish-orange rays rippled out toward us and dozens of stars began twinkling brilliantly in a very black sky - brilliant white jewels illuminating the night. The stars were brighter than I had ever seen.

"Look up there," Herbert interrupted. "Do you see that cluster of stars?" He pointed out the southern constellations as I followed the direction of his fingers. Then he ran out of galaxies to show me and turned to face me.

"I want you to be happy, and I will do anything I can to make you happy," he said.

I didn't answer at first. Then, a few seconds later, I stared down at my lap and said, "I know."

"You are free now. We don't have to listen to Nazi propaganda and we'll keep each other company until this war is over. We'll survive the war and celebrate with our families when it is over."

I looked down at the veins on my hands, at the way they traveled up from separate parts of my hand and flowed down to my finger tips. Things could come from separate directions, convene, and travel together.

"You will love it as much as I do," he said, "and if you don't, it will be like I told you. You will be free to go."

A hand reached across the seat for mine and hesitated. "My letters to you weren't words written on a sheet of paper, but the truth." He paused and collected himself. "If I count all the times I thought about you this past year, it would probably be several hundred times a day."

I had thought about him an equal number, all the while I worked for the Bathhursts and for the Harrisons. Herbert was all I thought about all those months in England, what kept me going, what gave me hope.

"I would whisper sweet words to you at night before I fell asleep, and hear myself calling your name when I was caught in a bad thought. If there were things to laugh about here, I wanted to share them with you, and if I needed advice, I asked you in my head. You're all I thought about this past year."

He pulled his hand back and stared down at it in his lap, quietly. The waves of the Congo lapped against the wooden pier, breaking against the stone pillars and through our silence.

"I'm in love with you Rosemarie," he said softly. "There have been other women in my life, but there is a deeper feeling for you than I have ever felt for anyone before, despite how difficult things have been."

I didn't know what to say. "Maybe we should go back," was what I did say.

That night, I slipped my nightgown over my head and carefully climbed inside the mosquito netting on Herbert's bed. I curled up on my side beneath the top sheet and then rolled over onto my back. When I did, I looked up and saw three bats hanging upside down on the netting, staring me in the face with their beady eyes and ghoulish wings. Bats flit around our yard in Bochum at night, but I had never seen them up close and I screamed, a curdling scream of horror.

In seconds, sofa springs creaked, a rescuer ran, and a door handle turned.

"Rosemarie, my beloved…"

Herbert set down his oil lamp in such a hurry that it almost fell over. Then he flailed against the netting with a broom. Wings fluttered, tiny monsters screeched, and then there was the grace of silence. Herbert had shooed them out the window. "They're gone," he said. "I forgot that they sometimes appear and it's all my fault. I promise that it will never happen again."

Herbert left and closed the door, but for a second, just a second, I wanted him to stay.

CHAPTER TWENTY-NINE

Herbert and Rosemarie

DAYS UNFOLDED with the warbling of birds and then slipped away wordlessly at dusk. I spent my days writing long letters to my family and counting the days until the next mail. I also read some of the books on Herbert's shelf and took a break to see Herbert typing letters to his parents. He slept on the couch in the evening, and in the morning, Ferdinand folded up the sheets and stored them in a closet, for the couch was used in Herbert's waiting room during office hours.

When I walked to the marketplace and returned all sweaty, I would retreat to the bathroom. That was the coolest place. I could turn the faucet on and let the cold water run over my fingers, and then I could haul out the wooden tray that Herbert had bought to fit over the tub. I would place some of the stationery I'd brought with me from Europe on top of the tray, along with a blue fountain pen. I placed them all on the dark tray and nestled it over the edge of the bathtub. Then I changed into a bathing suit and stepped into the bath, being careful not to splash any water on the stationery.

Instantly, I closed my eyes and sank back.

It had been awhile since I had heard from Tante Johanna, my mother's only sister. Tante Johanna was living all alone now, after losing her husband and her only child, Werner. My cousin Werner had died nine years ago, when I was 9 and he was only 21. He died of dysentery and my aunt wept at the funeral and for weeks afterwards. Then my Uncle Julius, a country doctor, died of pneumonia, and my aunt grew lonely in her Frankfurt villa. She sold her house, grieved as she packed up all the photographs of her husband and son, and moved to a smaller home where she took in two borders, other German Jews.

Poor Tante Johanna. I could close my eyes and see her now. The short wispy gray hair that reached only down to her ear lobes. The thick brows and soulful eyes. The pudgy white cheeks and double chin, and the broad, ample chest. I remembered every fold of her skin, and all the endearing words she had said to me in her latest letter, on a thin sheath of paper like Herbert had used. Tante Johanna's purple writing on the beige tissue paper was light and airy, but it belied unbearable sorrow.

My dear good Roslein,

Such joy you brought me with your dear letter and personal greeting! From your dear parents I hear that you are well and that you are happy and you are often in my thoughts.

I gave up my home and am staying in a guesthouse in order to live more economically. I had to do it because my income was greatly diminished, and since September I do not get a penny of rent from my house. The current place leaves much to be desired, but I have to resign myself to the inevitable.

My dear Roslein, from all my heart I wish you all the best. Do stay happy and content as you express in your letter and as it is also reported

194

from Bochum. If you and Herbert love each other, life's inevitable cliffs will be easier to surmount.

Make your own aunt happy and let me hear soon and in detail from you again. Bear in mind that I am greatly interested in everything which concerns you. From the bottom of my heart, good wishes.

Be lovingly hugged and kissed.

From your faithfully loving,

Tante Johanna

Many thanks for your own letter, Tante Johanna, I would write her. And, don't you worry about me. I'm fine and am getting used to my new life in Africa.

I was good at lying.

That afternoon, I saw Herbert walking toward me on the porch. He had said good-bye to a patient, which was probably his last one. There were fewer and fewer clients to care for because of his German accent and Germany's blitzkrieg through Poland. I pretended to read, but it was difficult to carry on that pretense with his shadow on my book.

"Let's go for a drive," he said, as I looked up to acknowledge him.

"A drive?"

"I've never shown you the gold mine where I work." He was the doctor for all the miners and their families, and he inspected the workers every month. "Would you like to go?"

I hesitated, looking out into the street, remembering the elephants, and then nodded. Maybe I would be able to see more African wildlife.

The trip to the gold mine was going to take two hours, and

the road wasn't paved. It was a dirt road carved out by tire tracks, with a hump of earth in the middle. We bounced along, scraping the bottom of Herbert's car on the clay bulge in the middle. The road was muddy, and there were puddles of water in the tire tracks the entire length of the trip. Water gathered every day during the rainstorms and never had a chance to dry out. The copper mud sprayed up from the puddles and splashed onto our hair and clothing.

When we reached the Congo River, Herbert drove our car onto a wooden raft and two natives rowed us across as Herbert and I leaned against his automobile and watched, trying to wipe some of the mud off my face and my once clean dress.

How am I going to survive in this wild place, I thought, as I looked at my mud-spattered dress and then the taut black muscles of our oarsmen, gliding us along on the pontoon. How am I going to learn how to love him?

Herbert drove the car off the pontoon and we journeyed on a short distance to the mine and a village of crude huts with thatched roofs. The miners' huts were no more than bare rooms with flattened earth floors. There were no beds or furniture, and not even a blanket in sight.

Outside, African men squatted down and stoked open fires while babies cuddled against their mothers' breasts. The men and women looked up at Herbert and smiled as we passed. "Yambo, mungaga," they said with a respectful nod and smile.

A little naked boy as tall as my thigh ran up and cocked his head to look at me. He smiled and I saw bright white teeth and a sparkle in his black eyes.

Another child, perhaps a sister, bounded forward and stood beside him. She reached out her hand and bashfully tugged at my skirt. I squatted down and she giggled and ran her brown fingers through my hair.

"They've never seen blonde hair before," Herbert explained.

"Jambo," I said to the little girl and she laughed. I thought she was impressed with my knowledge of Kiswaheli when Herbert smiled and corrected me.

"It's Yambo, not Jambo!"

"Yambo," I repeated and the little girl nodded. I twirled my right index finger in the air and gently tapped her naked belly. She giggled, displaying dainty white teeth.

I tickled her brother and he smiled.

"Mungaga," he said, pointing up at Herbert.

"Mungaga," Herbert nodded. Yes, he was a doctor.

A half dozen other children ran over toward us and stood back, shyly. They chattered in Kiswaheli and whispered to each other. I was beside myself, smitten from ear to ear.

"They are cute, aren't they," Herbert said.

The mothers and fathers of the children noticed Herbert and began carrying their sick ones toward us. Herbert led a line of villagers back to his car, where he opened up his black doctor's bag and spread his medical instruments on the front seat. Parents assembled to wait their turn, many with children in their arms as Herbert laid out his stethoscope, tongue depressors, thermometer, syringes and bandages.

There was an elderly man standing at the head of the line who was wearing a black shawl around his shoulders despite the summer heat. Herbert took his temperature and listened to his chest. "Unfortunately, I think this is pneumonia," Herbert said. I knew that was nearly a death sentence in Africa without medicine.

One man, who was bent over and leaning on a wooden cane, spoke to Herbert for several moments and seemed very appreciative.

"What did he say?" I asked Herbert, as the elderly man slowly walked away.

"He wanted to thank me for getting his prescription filled for atropine solution," Herbert said, closing up his black bag.

"Atropine solution? I don't understand."

"The man had severe diarrhea and needed medicine or he would have died. When I tried to fill his prescription at the pharmacy in Stanleyville, the pharmacist said that the medicine was unavailable. Of course the pharmacist had atropine, but he had instructions from the head office in Brussels not to give that medication to natives. The natives are viewed as subhuman and less worthy here."

"It's like Germany," I said.

"Exactly," Herbert said, "and I've had enough of that."

We looked out the car window at the miners and their families. "I love it here," Herbert said. "I love these people and these children."

I sighed, staring at an African woman sitting in the dirt outside her hut, with a naked baby sucking sleepy-eyed from her pear-shaped breast while another toddler squatted down and drew in the mud with a stick.

"It's all so foreign to me," I said. "At least I understood Germany. Here, I find the climate and the whole Colonial experience stifling." I told Herbert about the woman who had walked beneath me on the sidewalk. "For a native to have to get off the sidewalk because I'm white and she's African bothers me."

"But that's the way it is," Herbert said, fingering his car keys. "And maybe, if we stay here, we can be part of changing Africa to a more democratic way of life."

Herbert looked out at all the natives before starting up the car. "This is the country that gave me back my freedom after I lost it back home," he said. "I love it here, and I really want to stay. That is, if you do. I feel like I'm needed here, and I wasn't needed back in

Germany. I can do so much for these people and I want to."

His eyes were captivated by the little boy drawing in the soil. "I understand how difficult it is for you to get used to living here, but I think that if you give it a little more time you will learn to love it the way I do. Times are difficult right now, but they will get better. In the meantime, we have our freedom and the chance to help others."

Then Herbert turned and looked at me. "Rosemarie, your father wrote me as soon as he heard that we were married," he said, pulling a letter out of his shirt pocket. I recognized the stationery and felt a stab of pain at seeing the beautiful handwriting. Herbert handed the letter to me to read, and I could hear my father's voice.

Dear Dr. Molser,

I am hoping that I can give you my blessing and tell you that you're welcome as our son. Because I hope that I can have full confidence in you that you're going to be a true friend to our dear child and a good companion. In the high tide of feelings, remember that the boat of your life is in the throes of young life.

The whole world seems to be in glowing light, but there will come a time when the ship of your life goes into calmer waters and every day will come with many responsibilities. Then the high feelings of first love will change with what life expects of you and you will have to learn to be good to each other. You must learn to share worries and enjoyment and to let your companion in on your feelings. That gives life real value.

Just have an open heart for what is beautiful. Be interested and understand all the wonderful things in nature and in art. If you direct the ship of your life around those values, you will find that you can be successful and the shared journey can lead you to the heights of happiness. I wish you a wonderful journey.

Dein Vati

Herbert took a deep breath as my lower lip trembled and I struggled not to cry. "I love you Rosemarie," he said. "We spent a long time writing each other, and a year is long enough to know that we really love each other. Everything is going to work out all right, and you can have all the time you need."

Hitler continued with his tightening restrictions against the Jews and finally my parents could bear it no longer. They paid a farmer to smuggle them over the border to France in the back of his cattle wagon. They were hidden beneath a heavy blanket with Heidi between them as the wagon bounced up and down boulders and through the woods. My parents left our home and all of our possessions, taking with them only what they could hide and stuff in their coats.

In Portugal, my parents bought a boat ticket to America and fled Europe at last. But the joy of reunion with Margrit in America was very short lived. Father tried to eat better in the U.S. and regain his strength and spirit, but he remained in terrible pain. Then, the American doctors finally explained Vati's discomfort. He was suffering from cancer and it had been eating away at his stomach for years before traveling to his pancreas.

Of course my father's health hadn't been good, but his strong will helped him keep going and it gave me courage that he would get better. Now the news I dreaded most arrived. In a telegram, I learned that embracing my father at the train station was to be the last memory I would ever have of him because Father had died.

The telegram slipped through my fingers. Who would have thought that this would come to pass when I saw Father a year ago on the platform. We shook, fearing that our separation would be permanent, but we hoped that we would be wrong.

Vati even sounded like he had forgiven me in his last letter.

January 9, 1940

Dear Roselein,

I'm very sad today and I've got to share my thoughts with you. I think of all the years past when in the morning we came into your room with a new poem and a new song and showered you with gifts. Now you're no longer with us. Everything is gone and we only enjoyed you for a short time. You don't know how much I miss all of you. It's already almost two years since we said our good-bye to you and I can still see you sitting in the train and we were both shaking when we came to the border. How quickly the years flew by and now you have fled again to Africa. You don't know how much pleasure we get when we hear from you. As soon as we read your letter, we forwarded it on to Herbert's parents because they also need letters like they need their daily bread. It sounds like you have adjusted to life there in Africa.

Stay well, my dear Roslein. Be careful. I embrace you and love you.

Vati

How was it possible that I would never see my beloved father again? Never see him wheel the birthday cart into my room, eager to read his new birthday poem?

There was nothing fate could take from me that would hurt more than Vati. And of all the foolish things to do, fighting with Vati on the phone in England and in Belgium. I thought my parents would always be here and that there would be a chance for me to apologize. I thought I had all the time in the world to do that, and while I knew Father was sick, I didn't understand that he could die and slip away from me forever. Now I would never have the chance to say I was sorry to Father, and to ask him to understand why I had left England, coming here against his wishes. I would have to live with the guilt of disobeying him for the rest of my life.

Why was fate so mean?

I did not leave my bedroom for four days except to go to the bathroom. Ferdinand left trays of food outside the door in the morning, and scraped off the uneaten toast and papaya into the garbage in the afternoon.

Mutti,

Put a few flowers on my father's grave and tell him it's from Rosemarie. Stay well, because I've got to see you again. I take you in my arms and I kiss you and try to wipe your tears away. I hug you in my thoughts.

Rosemarie

I could not eat, and tears streamed down my face and onto my pillow. I had killed Father, I was sure of it, and I never even had a chance to say good-bye. My head was heavy with terrible, terrible feelings, and my mother's words were no comfort in her letter.

I know, my dearest Rosemarie, that you blame yourself for what happened to Vati, but I assure you, even in my own unending despair, that he would have died anyway. The cancer was obviously too far in its encroachment, and my poor heart is so sad. There is no anger inside me, only a longing for what used to be.

I love you and I hope you're happy with the man you married. I'm glad you have each other now. Remember what Vati said to me before you left? The roses are going to bloom again. We have to believe that.

I hug you through my own tears,
Mutti

Bloom again? My mother had lost more than anyone but I had lost the father who loved me so much. I had prayed to God every day and asked him to let me see my parents again and now my dream would never come true.

I didn't want to ever wake up.

On the fifth morning, the door to the bedroom creaked open and Herbert tiptoed in with a glass of papaya juice. I saw him out of the corner of my eye and watched him set the glass of juice down on the night table next to me, and then I felt the mattress sag.

Herbert's hand neatened my splayed hair and stroked my cheek softly where all the night's tears had fallen. New ones took their place, and his hand wiped them away and caressed me tenderly on the cheek.

"It's not your fault," Herbert said. "Your father was sick for a long time and you have got to stop blaming yourself. He had cancer and would have died whether you remained with him or not."

The tears fell harder and faster, and the hand was back like a dike. Then, Herbert pulled back the covers and helped me sit up on the side of the bed. He picked up the glass of juice he had set down and handed it to me.

"Here. Drink it. All of it. If you don't, you're going to get dehydrated in this heat and then your mother is going to be mourning the loss of two people she loves. I would be mourning, too."

I handed him back an empty glass.

I had been in Africa for just a few months, but I had come to see that trees and plants grow in the most impossible conditions. It's the heat and the humidity, Herbert once explained, as he pointed to a mango tree that had sprouted up through the water barrel outside our bathroom window. Nature was unpredictable and yet predictable. Thunderstorms, for instance, happened every afternoon. They were part of the daily rhythm of the Congo, and they were not only predictable but hauntingly beautiful.

It started with the smoky darkening of the sky, and soon the first eerie bolt ripped down from the heavens and illuminated the landscape. You could set your watch by it. In minutes, the sky boomed with a barrage of explosions. There were fifty or sixty of them, one every few seconds. Torrents of rain followed, and sheets of water kicked up clods of dirt.

Then, just like Herbert's mother was fond of saying in her letters, after every rain came sunshine. Thirty minutes after the thunderstorm, steam rose and you knew it was all over. You could walk outside and feel the heat rising. It was as hot as ever before the rain.

That night, there was an evening storm, and my heart pounded with every clap of thunder. It's just another storm, I said as I gazed out Herbert's bedroom at the flashes of the night. But, the bolts were striking too close for my liking, and the booming in the sky seemed even more deafening than I remembered.

I'm all alone here in Africa, I thought, mesmerized by the scene, staring at the spoonfuls of earth shooting up outside.

The separation from my family was so hard. Even though I had fought hard to come here, my greatest hope in life had been to see them and now I wondered if that would ever be possible. I would never see my father again, that was for certain, and would this war ever end so I could see my mother and sisters? Everything I ever loved was far away and yet...

I looked at the door to Herbert's bedroom which was closed as usual. Herbert was sleeping out in the living room on the sofa as he always did, giving me privacy. Out there in that living room was someone waiting to love me, if only I would let him.

I rubbed my wedding band on my left hand with my right finger and heard echoes. A snippet of a letter here, and another snippet there. I remembered one of the letters Herbert had sent me after I made the decision to come here.

My golden girl,
You would not be happy back in Germany or in England. I hate every bondage, but you will be free here. Free to choose what you want to do and when you want to give me your heart. I will not do anything you don't want me to do. But you will see, everything will turn out all right. The sun shines here for us like it does for everyone else, and that is not something we both had back in Germany. Do you understand?

I understood.

Leave your doubts in Europe my dear heart. We have lived for each other during the past few months. It was very often painful but now we have each other.

Each other. I nodded, admiring the gold band wrapped around my finger like a soul around a heart.

Our love for each other grew in our letters day by day, month by month and for more than a year. I spent many quiet hours at this typewriter. I've brought to you all my thoughts, my joys, my disappointments, and most of all my ever-growing love for my darling girl.

The storm finally ended and the scent of sweet mangoes filled the damp air. I pushed the door open to the living room a crack. There was a gorgeous full moon outside, and I could see a ray of moon light filtering onto the rug. It lit up the living room with a tender glow.

Herbert was sleeping on the sofa, lying on his side with his back to me beneath a blanket. He was wearing dark plaid pajamas, and his arm was curled under his head. He didn't stir.

I hovered over the slumbering figure for a few minutes, quietly watching. I stood there for a minute or two on the rug, gazing down at Herbert with an unexpected smile turning up at the corners of my mouth.

"Herbert," I whispered, but he didn't waken for I didn't say it loud enough for him to hear. I leaned over for a closer look at Herbert's peaceful, slumbering face, framed by his jet black hair and my eye caught the lovely dimple adorning his strong chin. What was it that I had disliked about Herbert when I first saw him?

I couldn't remember.

And then I realized that all those hundreds of letters Herbert had written me had come from his heart, to rescue me from danger and a war we had both foreseen. Herbert knew what was coming. There was a great deal of intelligence inside that mind of his, and Herbert had proven that he was genuinely concerned about me and that I could trust him. Every word Herbert had written to me this past year had been the truth. What more could he have possibly said or done?

Real love will make a bridge from one to the other, my mother had wisely written to me after she heard I got married. Father and I have learned to find our way to each other in love again after difficult times, and you will too.

I leaned over until my cheek was just a breath away from Herbert's, and then I kissed him ever so gently.

Herbert didn't stir, and then I did something quite unexpected.

I kissed him again.

The following morning, I slipped my hand into Herbert's as we walked together toward town. He turned to look at me and smiled, and I smiled back. Above us, there as a wide blue sky that stretched over the mango trees and as far as we both could see.

"You see that patch of blue?" my father had asked as he pointed up at a swatch of blue in a seemingly endless gray sky on one of our hikes back in Germany. "If it's big enough to make a handkerchief, we will have a beautiful day."

Walking alongside Herbert that morning, I saw that patch of blue.

EPILOGUE

After the war ended, Rosemarie and Herbert moved to New York where they reunited with Rosemarie's family. Soon after, the couple settled in Rochester, N.Y. where Herbert once again set up his medical practice in internal medicine and the couple raised two children. Rosemarie calls Herbert the love of her life. "He helped me grow up, and I helped him grow old," she said. The couple celebrated 61 years of marriage before Herbert died in 2000 at the age of 92.

Herbert was despondent over the fate of his own family. His parents, Hedwig and Georg Moses, took their own lives in Berlin in 1941 after receiving word that they would be deported "East," most likely to a concentration camp.

Rosemarie's parents and sisters are all gone now, and she and her nephew Peter are the sole survivors of the Marienthal family. Peter retired as vice president of The Hartford and lives in Connecticut and West Palm Beach, FL.

Rosemarie is not sure what happened to Suzi Zucker, and she may have survived the war. But, Tante Johanna Berg Franck, Uncle Phillip Guttentag, and Gert Freudenberg's parents were four of the six million Jews killed by the Nazis during the Holocaust. Tante Johanna died in Auschwitz and Uncle Phillip in Theresienstadt.

Both Rabbi David and Gert Freudenberg survived in England and remained there. Gert married and opened a stamp shop in London, but he changed his last name so it would no longer sound German or Jewish, and Rosemarie couldn't find him and never saw him again. But, she heard from a childhood friend that Gert never forgave himself for not being able to save his mother or father. With no way out of Germany, Hugo and Martha Freudenberg were rounded up and deported to Riga, the capital of Latvia. And there, in a nearby forest, in March 1942, they were shot with Bochum's remaining Jews.

Lilly Harrison and her family were Nazi victims as well. They were killed during a bombing of London.

When she was older, Rosemarie was reunited with her girlhood friends Inge, Doris and Crystal who told Rosemarie that they rode their bikes past her house many times after she was expelled from school, hoping to catch a glimpse of her. But, they were afraid to knock on her door or be seen with her, because it was dangerous to be friends with a Jew.

She now understands, Rosemarie says. "I don't hate anybody anymore," she said recently. "To be honest, what happened to my family doesn't hurt so much anymore. We were lucky, and we got out. We have to be grateful for what happened, because if I hadn't left Germany, I would never have met Herbert. And, I wouldn't have gone to America, and I love America."